Saving Will

Ryan Webb

ISBN 978-1-63784-807-4 (paperback)
ISBN 978-1-63784-808-1 (digital)

Copyright © 2025 by Ryan Webb

All rights reserved. No part of this publication may be reproduced, distributed, or transmitted in any form or by any means, including photocopying, recording, or other electronic or mechanical methods without the prior written permission of the publisher. For permission requests, solicit the publisher via the address below.

Hawes & Jenkins Publishing
16427 N Scottsdale Road Suite 410
Scottsdale, AZ 85254
www.hawesjenkins.com

The following is fiction, except for the parts that aren't.

Printed in the United States of America

To my family, for their amazing support.
To the family and friends of Eric M. Didocha.

5/16/17

Dear Dad,

    I need to sit down and write you this letter, which I fear may turn into the length of a book. You can believe whatever you want from this, and I know you'll disbelieve much of it. But I've let that stop me from writing this for over a decade, and I've decided that I don't care about that anymore. I don't need to convince you of anything. I just need you to read. This is about the darkest and most confusing time of my life—a time you remember well, but also a time in which no one knows the whole strange truth. I'm not sure why I've decided on you as my target audience for the rest of this story. Maybe that will become clear to me as I get these words out. Maybe not.

    It's the story of my best friend, William Eli Hogan. Will—of course—as you and I and everyone else call him. It's hard to say where the story starts, though I now know where it ends. I won't forget any of this for as long as I live, but I'll start with the singular moment of the whole thing that is carved into my very being to this day, thirteen years later.

    I was at an appointment with a customer in Dearborn, trying to concentrate on my sales pitch while fighting off the pit in my stomach caused by my cell phone repeatedly buzzing in my pocket, signaling one text message or missed call after another. When your best friend has been in a medically induced coma for a week, every time the phone buzzes even once, you get a surge of scared electricity shooting through your body. But when it taps at your leg repeatedly in a ten-minute period, you could almost vomit.

So, after my counterpart Terrance and I shook hands with our customer and stepped into the hall, I tentatively pulled my phone out of my pocket to see a text message from my friend Randy, simply asking, "Is what I'm hearing true?" and three missed calls from Will's brother, Alex, three years my senior, but also my fraternity brother from our days at Mitchel College. No messages. Terrance stood next to me as I leaned against a table in the hall of the busy hospital and called Alex back.

He didn't say hello. He picked up and, through sobs, told me that Will was brain dead. "He was supposed to make it," Alex cried. "He was supposed to live. This wasn't supposed to happen. I can't believe this is happening."

What do you say to that? I couldn't say much. I can barely write this now without crumbling under decade-old grief. In fact, I don't recall *what* I said. I'm sure I was quiet and supportive as I tried to swallow the acorn-sized lump in my throat in the hallway and fight back a meltdown outside the hospital auditorium.

I *do* remember hanging up and turning toward the auditorium, hoping no conference was being held, collapsing in the first seat I found, and crying harder than I had ever before or since. I remember Terrance putting his arm around my back and telling me about a high school football player he once knew—or something like that—who died young, and that because of that, he understood how I was feeling. That comment is the reason I never say things like that to others in times of deep grief. How could he have any inkling of how I was feeling? He couldn't. I was spinning, sinking, shaking, and wanting to throw up all at once. I had never known before how *physical* grief could be. It got physical when, four weeks after your best friend stood next to you wearing a rented tux—flashing a happy but mischievous grin for your wedding photographer—he was gone. And in that time before digital photography, Ann and I hadn't even *seen* the photos yet, and he was gone. No, that was not supposed to happen.

The flashes of us the month before in our tuxes snapped me back.

I have to call Ann. How do I tell her?

I needed her in that moment, and I wished she was with me. I hugged Terrance and thanked him. I'm grateful for him to this day; he is why I wasn't alone when hearing the worst news of my life. I struggled from the auditorium to the parking structure, feeling like my legs were on backward and wondering how all the people in the halls and atrium of the medical center could go about the day as if nothing had happened. I staggered up the stairs to the third level of the deck, melted into the Grand Prix's driver's seat, took one deep breath, and dialed my newlywed wife.

"Are you driving?" I asked her when she picked up.

"Yeah."

"Please pull over when it's safe."

"Okay."

At that point, I probably didn't even need to use words to tell her what had happened. She had been on high alert for the past week since the accident, just as I had been, and my call, my tone, and my ominous request were all she would have needed. But she parked at a restaurant, and through laboring breaths and salty tears, I told her the news anyway. After briefly exchanging our anguish over the phone, we agreed to meet between Dearborn and Royal Oak, so she could drive us to the hospital in Ann Arbor to see Will's family and Will if we could.

The last thing Alex said to me on the phone that afternoon was that his mom wanted me to call all of Will's friends to tell them the news. As you know, he was the guy who counted no fewer than fifteen people who considered him one of their *best* friends and probably fifty more who would say he was a very good buddy. The tuxedo he rented for our wedding the month before was one of *three* tuxes he rented for groomsman duties during just a four-week period that summer, and there had been many more in previous years. There would be a few later that year for which the rental order was placed, but the tux would never be picked up. That said, having the job of calling around to break this news to so many people Will was so close with was hell for me. Each time I was able to regain my composure, it was time to say goodbye to someone and start the brutal news all over again with someone else. I was reliving the pain of my phone call with Alex on a repeating ten-minute-long loop as Ann drove us to where Will lay with no brain function and machines keeping his systems operating.

Ann parked her Ford Escape in the same lot we'd parked in most nights during the previous week when we prayed for him to emerge from a coma. Turning to me, she asked, "Are you ready?"

"No," I replied, despite reaching for the door handle and stepping into the June air.

Collapsing my six-foot, three-inch frame around Will's tiny Italian American mother in the family waiting area of the Critical Care Unit, I flashed to her phone call eight days prior. It was Father's Day, and I had fallen asleep on my couch watching the US Open golf tournament, nursing a mild hangover from a post-soccer-game celebration the night before in Petoskey, before heading over to see you and mom in the early evening to celebrate your day. He was the kind of friend who was so close that his parents' cell numbers were programmed into your phone, so I knew it was her before I sleepily picked up.

"The police just came to our house," she said, not crying but obviously shaken and speaking in short bursts. "Will's been in an accident. They say it might be pretty bad. We are on our way to the hospital now. He's unconscious. I'm freaking out right now. He's my baby, RJ. I called you and Marcus—you guys tell everyone else. Tell them to pray. Just tell them to pray."

I didn't say much—just to keep me posted on updates when they got to the hospital. Before I called Marcus to compare notes, I sat back and wondered if maybe she was overreacting. I know how parents can do that when it comes to the safety of their children. But the police came. That's like something you see in the movies. So, I started making phone calls, the first of what would be many over the next week and a half.

Now there I was, eight days after taking that call from Mrs. H and many visits to Will's bedside, hugging his mom, surrounded by stunned sorrow. After fifteen minutes of embraces and weak-in-the-knees sobbing, everyone other than Mr. and Mrs. H were asked to step out of the closed-door portion of the larger family waiting area so they could meet in private with a representative from Gift of Life organ donation. I was too consumed with grief to think much about this meeting and its significance, and I certainly had no concept of the events that would domino from this private conversation.

*****

  You and mom were at the funeral, so you know how packed that room was—like nothing I've ever seen. He was really "that guy," wasn't he? Only a couple of people spoke as part of the planned service—with his brother-in-law-to-be speaking so beautifully—and then they opened it up to anyone else for comment. I couldn't move. I felt eyes looking at me. I knew exactly what I was going to say—what I *would* say. But I was frozen. Like I said, grief can be physical. A week later, I sent Will's mom a card and wrote exactly what I would have said if I could have. It helped me get it out, but I still felt guilty that I couldn't say it in front of hundreds of mourners.

  After finally regaining movement when they motioned for the pallbearers to move to the front of the room, I took my last look at my best friend before they closed the casket. He wore a suit and tie and a baseball cap from his high school playing days. Some, on that day, thought it was a piece of nostalgia to accompany a twenty-six-year-old taken from this earth too soon. Those of us who spent the last week in the hospital with Will while he was in a medically induced coma knew that the hat also served to hide the severe head injury he suffered. When we saw the hat, we also envisioned the SUV, carrying him and all his possessions from his Chicago apartment to his parents' Detroit-area home on Father's Day, coming upon an unexpected traffic stoppage, careening off the side of the highway, rolling four times, and finally resting next to a state trooper's vehicle.

  After loading Will's body into the hearse, we got into one of the lead cars and silently drove the three miles to the two-hundred-acre cemetery visible from I-75. After winding through countless turns, we finally arrived at his final resting place and looked back to see the string of vehicles behind us stretched so far that it went throughout the entire meandering cemetery and onto the two main roads leading to the cemetery—about a two-mile-long bumper-to-bumper chain. I used to get upset when I got stuck at a traffic light because we all had to wait for an extensive funeral caravan; I've never looked at them the same. Only special people have lines that long. Once everyone settled in, the clergyman discussed Will's place in the afterlife before the casket was lowered into the ground. They didn't start throwing dirt on it like in the movies. That was it. We all just slowly started parting ways. This part of every funeral I've ever attended has felt weird. It's like I feel there should be something else. I don't know—something said, something done. But there's really nothing left *to* do. So everyone goes his or her own way.

I know you and Mom loved Will too. I know you were both there for most of that final day, and I appreciate you being there with me. Your memories may differ from mine, and that's okay. Frankly, I expect that at this point. I only write these details so you can see them through my eyes and so we're on the same page about the reality of that day because, a week later, my reality started to part ways with yours. And I'm quite sure everyone else's too.

*****

Understatement time: the following week was difficult. The same feeling nagged at me—walking around, wondering how everyone else around me didn't know what was going on inside my head and didn't feel the emptiness on the verge of tears I felt every minute. I passed people laughing with one another in the halls about some unknown previous joke.

Didn't they know?

The rest of the world had the audacity to continue and leave me behind in a fog. At a one-on-one meeting with my fifty-something boss, he shared that his brother was hit by a car and killed when he was a teen. He seemed so matter-of-fact about this.

"How long did it take you to recover?" I asked.

"Oh, a long time, of course. I still think about him, but it is easier now."

"I just can't imagine ever…"

"You will go from thinking about your friend every second of the day to every minute, then every hour, then every day, and then there will come a time when, at some point, each month or so you will see or hear something that will remind you of him. The difference, too, is that when you get to that stage, more often than not, you'll smile in these moments rather than tear up. I know that's hard to believe now, but it's true for me, and I bet it will be true for you."

It *was* hard to believe. I don't know what the proper order of grieving is that I hear people reference, but I know that for me, that week after the funeral, while I was still very sad, I was also very angry. I was mostly angry with God. Growing up, you and I literally never talked about God once, even *conceptually*. But after falling in love with a cute Christian girl, I started really trying. I approached it with my headfirst, hoping my heart would follow. I listened at church on Sundays (and read and asked questions on other days), like I was in a college class and every bit of it would be on the final exam. I learned a lot, and I'd say my heart was starting to follow—not a good time in that process to have something seemingly so senseless like this happen.

I was pissed at all the people at the funeral who said, "He's in a better place."

Really? Better than being a fun-loving twenty-six-year-old with countless good friends and a great family he was moving back to?

I felt like the God talk at the service was just to make the rest of us somehow feel better, more so than a description of reality. If there was a God, how on earth could he take Will away from us like that? With all the evil people in the world, why would God take a young man who was such a good person away from us? I was pissed with those who told me, "Everything happens for a reason."

Really? What reason could this be?

It sure seemed to me that any purpose for this paled in comparison to the purpose Will could have had for his life. Just think about all he could have done.

The year prior, I had read Mitch Albom's book, *The Five People You Meet in Heaven*, and one evening that week, I broke down again with Ann and said to her, "If there are only five people you meet in heaven, Will better be one of them for me." That same night, I lashed out in anger at another five people I'd never met. I muttered, "Those five people who got Will's organs…I don't think they'll ever realize what they have. They better damn well live the most amazing lives from here on out, because Will would have had such a cool life. They better do something with this." I sobbed, barely breathing through tears and gritted teeth. "They better do something because this wasn't supposed to happen."

On the Sunday after the Monday funeral, Ann and I had our usual post-church brunch at Max & Irma's Restaurant. When we got back to the condo, I was drained, so I went into the lower level to crash on the couch. I can't say how long I slept because this is the part of my letter where timelines get fuzzy. My phone's ringer jolted me out of my nap. I thought I'd put it on silent mode. The caller ID indicated it was from Mr. and Mrs. Hogan's house. *Mrs. H must have gotten my card with the words I wished I had said at the funeral*, I thought.

"Hello," I said sleepily.

"Wake up, dude," a man's voice said. But it wasn't Mr. H's voice, and he wouldn't talk like that anyway.

"Huh? Haha. Who is this?"

"So I move away for a few years and you delete my home phone number from your contacts?"

"Wha—What? What is this? Who is this?

"Man, you *are* still asleep. It's Will. I just called from my parent's home phone cuz my phone died in the car, so it's charging."

It was. I couldn't speak. I mean, you'd think I would have immediately thought it was a prank, but as soon as he said, "It's Will," I knew it was him.

I stammered, "But. You. Are you okay?"

"Yeah, I'm good. I left a little earlier than planned to beat the Sunday night traffic from people heading home from their Lake Michigan cottages."

I was definitely awake, but what was I experiencing? I closed my eyes and opened them again, as if this would help me gain clarity. When I reopened them, the TV was coming back from a commercial, showing the US Open final day leaderboard.

He continued, "So did you get my message last night while you were up in Petoskey?"

The message! I'd been beating myself up over deleting a voicemail message since first learning of Will's accident from his mom. When I was at the bar with the soccer team celebrating our victory, Will called me, but I didn't pick up because it would have been too loud to hear anything. As we spilled out of the bar and tumbled into the back of our designated driver's car, I listened to Will's voice in his usual mischievous way say, "Hey, hey. Just calling to say what's up…and that I talked to Ann, and she told me to say she loves you. See ya!" he closed with a funny voice. I found out later that he had tried my home phone first—remember when people did that?—and found out from Ann that I was at the tournament. I doubt she said, "Call him on his cell and tell him I love him." But that was just Will—always a playful smart aleck but often in a way some would describe as sweet. The message was only a few seconds long, and I knew the real reason he was calling was to confirm getting together for a beer on Monday night to celebrate his homecoming, so I quickly deleted the message and went to bed. Of all the voicemail messages I've received, that's the one I most regret deleting. These days, I'm sure there would be an easy way to recover it; back then, I wasn't aware of one if it existed. I had spent two weeks stewing over it. And of all the missed calls I've ever had, that's the one I most wish I had picked up.

"Yeah…I got it."

"So you still good for beers tomorrow after work?"

"Um, yeah. You're okay? I mean…"

"Yeah, better question: are *you* okay? You still sound like you haven't woken up from that nap."

"I'm fine now. I'm looking forward to seeing you tomorrow, Will."

He must have been taken aback by the formality and weight of that last phrase because he laughed and then said his signature phrase, "Cool, cool," and added, "See you at Gelston Bar at nine."

I know this sounds dumb because I'm writing you a *letter*, but I don't know words to describe what I was feeling when we hung up. I was certainly confused, scared, and happy all at once. I just stared at the TV, watching Retief Goosen make one clutch putt after the next. As you well know, the US Open only comes once a year. This was the golf event from two weeks prior—Goosen topped Phil Mickelson by two strokes. I was back to Father's Day, and Will was alive, and I had just spoken to him on the phone. In the movies, they wonder if maybe they were dreaming, so they pinch themselves or whatever. But it wasn't like that; I knew I was awake and that what had just happened really *happened*.

After several minutes of silent sitting, I called Ann, who was on her way home from the gym. I didn't really know how to start, so I think I said something like, "Hey, honey. Is everything okay?"

"Yeah, just left a little bit ago. I'm almost home. Why? What's going on?"

"Um, I just got a phone call…from *Will*." I braced myself for her response.

"Oh, yeah. That's tomorrow night you guys are getting together, right? I assumed that's why he called last night when you were up north."

She didn't know. She didn't know about his accident, his week-long coma, or his death. I just couldn't wrap my head around what I was experiencing. How was she not surprised by his call?

"Yeah, that's tomorrow night." I tried not to say much else, for fear she might think her husband of one month was losing his mind. The next twenty-four hours were like an out-of-body experience or something. We visited you and Mom as planned, only this time we focused on the US Open conclusion on the garage TV while tending the grill rather than quietly discussing Mrs. Hogan's startling phone call and what might come of Will.

How does no one else know this? What is *this?*

SAVING WILL

I went through the motions of everything I did, just thinking about the call and looking forward to the next evening.

*****

We met at Gelston Bar at 9:00, just as we had planned. We exchanged the usual "bro hug," but I held on for an extra beat.

"Easy there, big fella," Will joked, "it hasn't been *that* long."

"It's just...good to see you" was all I could think to say, fighting back tears, trying not to totally freak out, and wondering if I should say anything about my past reality—and *how* to say it.

We grabbed a beer at the bar and found a booth. He talked about how he'd miss Chicago but how happy he was to get home to Detroit, where his parents and three siblings all lived. He asked how married life was treating me. This was the first time seeing him since my wedding, so we reminisced about the day and laughed about our buddy, Sam, walking out of the reception hall carrying enough "last call" drinks to last until breakfast. (Thanks again for picking up the bar tab that night.) Well, this was the first time seeing him since the wedding, if you didn't count me seeing him unconscious and hooked up to all the stuff in the hospital for a week and then in the casket with his baseball hat. At that point, I wasn't sure what counted.

Sitting in our corner booth, I pointed to the faint number eight shaved into his hairy forearm and cracked up. As you know, Will was one of the hairier guys around, so seeing a figure eight in his arm was hilariously visible. It was really surreal, because I had just told the story of the eight to his mom at his bedside in the hospital. In February, before the accident, Ann, Will, and I went up north to visit another fraternity brother, Alan, and go skiing. After a long day on the slopes, we played cards and had a few—okay, maybe more—adult beverages at Alan's place in the woods. Will and I made fun of Alan's NASCAR fandom, and when Will could tell he was getting under someone's skin, he went all out. He told Alan he was going to capture his girlfriend's new cat and shave the number 88 into his back so he could be a "Real Dale, Jr. Fan." After stern words from all involved parties, Will and I found our opportunity, snagged the skinny gray cat, and locked ourselves in the bathroom.

"Don't you dare, you SOBs!" Alan slurred from the other side of the door.

We, of course, couldn't stop laughing. Will found Alan's electric shaver and fired it up. The yelling from outside got louder. I wasn't sure if Will was really going to do it. He was mischievous but never malicious, and after the shaver started loudly humming, it was clear Alan was serious. We could have just kept the shaver running for a while to mess with Alan, but Will's commitment to messing with his friends was deeper than that, so he decided that in order to really sell the idea that we were shaving an "88" into the cat's back, he would shave his own hairy arm. Like I said, total commitment. Alan freaked out when the sound of the shaver changed, and it was clear that it was actually cutting hair, shouting profanities at us, and violently jiggling the bathroom door handle. Will meticulously made a perfect figure eight in his left forearm. He stopped before doing another one with his other arm to complete the task. We let the still fully-follicled cat out of the bathroom, much to Alan's relief, and laughed until it hurt at Will and his redesigned arm.

Snapping back to my new reality, over the increasing noise at Gelston Bar, I said, "I just told your mom the story of why you have that—she didn't know about it."

"When did you talk to my mom?"

"Oh…um…I don't remember. Sometime within the last few months, I guess, since we freaked out Alan—and his girlfriend's cat."

What I didn't tell Will was that at his coma bedside, I had pointed to the faint "8" outline and managed a chuckle. Mrs. H said she had wondered what that was, so I told her the story, and she smiled for the first time that day, shook her head, and said, "That's my Will, all right."

After several more stories and laughs, Will decided one beer was enough and that it was time to get home because he had to move into his new apartment the next day. I wanted to stay longer. I felt like I was getting what I'd wanted for the week since we buried him—one more chance.

But I didn't want to freak him out, and I certainly didn't want to try to explain everything I'd experienced—or *thought* I'd experienced—in the last few weeks. We walked out to the parking lot and started to part ways.

Will said, "I'll call you about helping me move the furniture whenever I figure out when I'm gonna get it from my brother."

"Okay. I'm ready to help you any way I can, man. It is really good to have you back, Will."

"Cool, cool."

Another bro hug, and off we went.

*****

As Ann and I stood brushing our teeth that night, I considered how I might tell her what was going on. It was so hard not to talk to anyone. But she didn't seem fazed by Will being back; in fact, in her reality, he never left. As I spit out toothpaste, I decided I was just content knowing Will was alive and that maybe someday I would figure out how this all happened—maybe seek professional help to see if I had experienced some sort of alternate reality psychosis, if there was such a thing.

I fell asleep quickly that night, likely exhausted from the emotions of the last several hours, but it didn't last long. I was jolted awake by my cell phone ringing, with the caller ID indicating it was the Hogan house. "Now what?" I thought, my heart hammering my chest.

"Hello?"

"It's Mrs. H. Will's been in an accident," the voice said breathlessly. "Hit on his way home from seeing you, I think. It sounded like a guy ran a red light and plowed into the side of his car. We're on our way to the hospital now."

Now crying, she added, "They said it's bad, RJ. He's unconscious. I'm freaking out right now. He's my baby. I called you and Marcus—you guys tell everyone else. Tell them to pray. Just tell them to pray."

In a trance, I think I just grunted that I would spread the word and that I would pray.

How?

Confusion quickly gave way to guilt.

I was with *him. I could have done something. I could have stayed with him until he was home.*

Against everything I knew to be true, I had my best friend back, and then I just let him go. After I shared the news with Ann, the two of us sat up in bed crying over Will—she, experiencing this for the first time, and I, inexplicably, for my second.

*****

The next couple of weeks were like living in a remake of a movie that was just a little *off* from the original. I made the same daily trips to the hospital just as I had before, I received the same horrible, memorable phone call from Will's brother to tell me he was brain dead ("This wasn't supposed to happen"), and I watched the same miles-long line of cars crawl into the cemetery, where my best friend was again buried in the ground wearing his high school baseball cap.

The brutality of it all was unspeakable. To go through it for the first time was bad enough, but to have to do it again was a personal hell. My sleep was miserable, and my grip on my mental health was quickly slipping. I again wondered if I was experiencing some sort of prolonged hallucination. One night, I had such a vivid dream it took me being awake fifteen minutes to fully determine I hadn't actually seen it. In the dream, there was a tall, thick oak tree in my backyard with several crappy-looking plants or trees all around it. A flock of about seven sheep grazed on grass in the yard until the smallest one looked up at the oak tree, walked up to its base, and began to chew away its bark. It chewed faster and faster, with wood dust and clumps of bark falling to the grass below. I watched with dread as the sheep chewed through enough of the tree that it came violently crashing down, narrowly missing me as I jumped out of the way. The entire flock fixed their eyes on me, then all turned in the direction of the one who chewed the tree. In that moment, the smaller plants and trees perked up and started rapidly growing in a time-lapse style. The sheep all turned back to stare at me again, but more intensely, like they were angry with me. I woke up terrified, sweating, and clutching my chest.

*****

After work that day, I connected with Will's brother, Alex, for coffee. As you know, I've never been one for coffee, but with the way I had been sleeping, I needed it in the late afternoon to even stay up past dinner time. Our conversation was as you might expect, with both of us vacillating between "barely keeping it together" and "not quite keeping it together."

"How's your mom holding up? I mean, I can't even..."

"She's as you would expect, which is pretty bad," Alex managed through a cracking voice.

I mean, how could I tell him what I had experienced? I had a second chance to see him one last time, and maybe I had a chance to save him.

"Yeah, I sent your folks a card with the words I would have said at the funeral if I had been able to."

"She mentioned that. I know it meant a lot to her. You know, Will loved you like a brother, so my mom thinks of you as one of her own."

"I loved Will too, man. I..." couldn't finish the sentence. I thought of my *actual* brother, and it made me want to call Drew just to hear his voice.

"She said the Gift of Life people contacted my parents to see if they would have interest in meeting any of the donor recipients, you know, from Will's...donation."

"What're they gonna do?"

"I dunno. I don't know if that would help or hurt right now. It's just crazy to think about part of him...I can't even...just part of him still being alive."

I paused before saying, "Yeah. Weird to think about, for sure."

I thought about my raging comment to Ann when Will died, about the five recipients of his organ donations needing to be saints to make up for us losing Will at twenty-six. Until the coffee conversation, the idea of these five people was just that—an idea. I had never actually thought of the real people on the other end of this strange, tragic-for-some transaction. What were their stories? What were they going to do now? Did they know Will's story? Did they even *want* to know? All of this came quickly to me at Starbucks that day.

"Well, maybe it would help. I dunno" was the best I could come up with. The conversation didn't go far after that. Just two guys in their late twenties staring at our coffees, trying to silently lean on each other even though neither of us could stand much on our own.

*****

A week later, the proofs from our wedding photos were ready to be picked up. On what is, for most people, a joyful occasion, looking through our photos was painful. There was Will, who was very much alive. Looking at these photos, I could hear his laugh and his wise cracking during all the poses the photographer put us through. There was the one where he and Drew grabbed my arm as if to stop me from going into the church to go through with the ceremony. That brought me right back to when Drew came to our condo the night before the funeral. He was being a supportive brother, and I appreciated it, but it wasn't until he stepped into my condo and wouldn't let go of my normal greeting hug as he sobbed into my chest that I realized how impacted he was by Will's death. It made sense, though. While many friends treated Drew like the little brother five years my junior with a pat-on-the-head approach, Will treated him as a peer. That's just how he was, as you know. He made everyone feel important. Valued.

Then there was the photo when Will must not have heard the photographer's instructions because, while all the groomsmen were huddled in a circle looking down at the photographer lying on the ground, Will was the only one who was not smiling. It wasn't an upset look or even a serious look. That's what made that photo haunting.

Looking at it felt like Will was looking at me in that moment, saying, "Enough with all these cheesy smiles."

I couldn't take much of it, honestly. I broke down quickly and felt horrible, as I was ruining our marital moment, but Ann was—of course—very supportive. It was then she suggested I consider "talking to someone," which was code for therapy. Little did she know I was thinking about more serious "talking" based on my nonreality reality situation with seeing Will again, only to lose him again. I told her I would think about it. We set aside the photos and went to bed.

*****

Thanks for bearing with me here, Dad. I realize this note is getting lengthy, but there is a lot more to the story, and I must keep going to get this all out—it's helping me to finally write it all down.

Early in the morning, after the impossibly emotional wedding photos review, my cell phone buzzed, breaking me out of the little sleep I was able to grab that night. Except I wasn't in my bed and my phone wasn't on the nightstand. I was on a blow-up mattress on the floor, and my phone was on a coffee table next to me. And the caller ID was Will's cell phone.

"Hello?"

"Yo, did I catch you still asleep?"

It was Will again.

"Hey! I was sleeping. I mean, after we looked at the photos, we…went to bed…but…"

"Dude, you all right?"

Here it went again: me trying to get my bearings out of a dead sleep, talking to my dead best friend.

"I'm fine. Just confused. You're…back," I said, part statement, part question.

"Well, I'm still in Chicago—gonna take off around noon."

I finally looked at my surroundings. I was on the floor of a friend's living room in Northern Michigan, the guy who hosted us for that soccer tournament on Father's Day weekend. It was the morning of Will's accident. Again.

"Don't leave at noon!" I blurted out.

"Huh?"

"I mean. Leave earlier if you can. I will meet you when you get to town, and we can grab a bite or something."

"I thought we were grabbing a beer tomorrow night."

"Right. But can we switch it up and do it tonight instead?"

"Yeah, but it's Father's Day, and I was hoping to hang out with my folks tonight."

"Okay, right. If you make it...I mean, maybe after dinner, I'll come over. If that's cool with your parents."

"That should be fine. I'll text you later to let you know what time and if plans change."

"Okay. I'll see you soon."

"Cool, cool."

After we hung up, I developed a clear mission. I was going to save Will. I was likely the only one who could. If this was going to be like the other time he came back, I was going to be the only one experiencing his very *presence* as a chance to save his life. I jumped off the half-deflated air mattress, tried to shake off the morning-after-bar-celebration cloud, got dressed, and grabbed my car keys to make the four-hour drive home.

Halfway home, I called you and mom to let you know I was stopping by a little earlier than planned to celebrate Father's Day. As we sat in the shade on the deck, I didn't say anything about what was happening with me, my repeating reality, my mission to save my best friend, or my gripping anxiety the entire time we talked, and I wondered if Will would make it home safely this time. You had the US Open on the TV in the garage as you always do on Father's Day, and as we checked the progress of the ribs on the grill, we watched Phil Mickelson three-putt from five feet away on the seventeenth to go from leader to trailer.

"There goes Phil, missing another short putt," you said.

"Yeah, he always misses that same putt," I replied, realizing the irony of my comment, considering I had seen him miss this *exact* putt before—*literally*.

Wait, that putt. I've seen that putt. That putt happens (happened?) after Mrs. Hogan woke me up from my nap with the news of the accident. That must mean Will hasn't gotten into the accident. Leaving an hour early—as I suggested—may have gotten him home safely.

I had to find out, so I texted him to see if he made it home safely. I didn't want to freak him out, so I played it cool with a regular "u home?" message. Then I waited. After witnessing Goosen finish off Phil by two strokes, we ate on the picnic table and cleaned up our bony mess. I still hadn't heard back from Will. As I glanced at my phone repeatedly, Mom could tell I was preoccupied and said, "I'm sure he's just having dinner with his family, and he's being polite and not replying."

"Yep, I'm sure that's what it is," I said, not at all sure that's what it was.

Having still not heard a response, I headed home to see Ann, who was on her way home from her parents' house. As I pulled into the garage, my phone rang. "Hogan House" appeared on the caller ID.

He made it!

"Yo," I said.

"The police just came to our house," said Mrs. Hogan—not crying, but obviously shaken and speaking in short bursts. "Will's been in an accident. They say it might be pretty bad. We are on our way to the hospital now. He's unconscious. I'm freaking out right now. He's my baby, RJ. I called you and Marcus—you guys tell everyone else. Tell them to pray. Just tell them to pray."

"No. This can't be. He left earlier."

"Wha-what?"

"I mean…I don't know what I mean. I'm scared and confused."

"Me too, RJ. I have to go. Just pray."

"Okay, please keep me posted."

And with that, she was gone. I sat in the garage with my forehead on the steering wheel, wondering how this could have happened again. The original accident—at least the one I experienced in my first reality—happened because he came upon a construction zone on the highway where a line of cars had stopped unexpectedly. A state trooper witnessed Will come up to the backup, not speeding, but having to swerve to the right shoulder to avoid hitting the car in front of him, only to have his front right wheel go off the shoulder and onto the grass. He swung the wheel back to the left to avoid going into the gully, but the weight of the SUV loaded with all of his belongings sent the vehicle into a barrel roll on the shoulder—four times before coming to a rest—and amazingly, he did not hit any of the cars stopped on the road. But leaving an hour early should have changed this reality. I thought the same backup shouldn't be there because the traffic would be different.

The traffic may have been different, but the outcome of the day was the same: my best friend was clinging precariously to life in a hospital bed, his head swollen nearly beyond recognition.

*****

The "coma week," as I began to call it in my head, was a brutal do-over for me, while obviously fresh and raw for everyone else. You'd think the repeat nature of this dark time would have made it easier for me given that I could brace myself for what I knew was coming, but it didn't. It was worse *because* I knew what was coming. The hope—and likely some ignorance—I had had during my initial experience of his coma gave way to the resignation of someone who already knows how a movie ends. I tried, but this made it tougher for me to be the cheerleader the family probably needed during this time because, of course, they *didn't* know how the movie was going to end. On top of the grief, I was now under a blanket of guilt. *This* time—or whatever I could call this as I tried to grasp what I was experiencing—there was something I could have done to prevent everyone's pain.

I could have done more. I could have driven to Chicago to pick him up. I could have somehow communicated what I knew.

SAVING WILL

In the family waiting area, I sat with Will's dad while he went through Will's cell phone contacts list and called out the names of people he didn't know. Some of this was nervous energy needing to find release while taking breaks between visits to Will's room, where he lay unconscious, but it was also about Mr. Hogan learning a bit about his son's sense of humor as we laughed at some of the nicknames he'd given his phone contacts—some names the recipients would like, others we agreed to keep between us. Never malicious, always mischievous. The sheer number of names on that phone was baffling but shouldn't have been, given Will's ability to befriend seemingly anyone.

"Neil Whitaker?" Mr. Hogan questioned.

"Yep, one of the guys we graduated with," I replied.

Given Will's end-of-life state, that name immediately took me back to a conversation he, Neil, and I had in my dorm room one night during our sophomore year. Neil was good-looking and leveraged that with many women in our first year of college. And he partied hard. In our sophomore year, his roommate was a Christian guy with several "preachy" Christian friends, and this—combined with the summertime loss of his uncle, who experienced a death bed conversion—led to a big change in Neil's life. He gave up drinking, settled down the promiscuity—although forever his weakness—and actually gave his faith testimony on stage in front of hundreds of his fellow students. I wasn't sure how "legit" all of this was, but it was what led Neil, Will, and I to discuss the afterlife during a study session in my room.

"So let me get this straight. Even if I'm a good guy, I don't kill anyone, I'm nice to people, etc. I'm not necessarily going to heaven?" I questioned.

Neil hesitated. "Yeah," he said apologetically. "The only way to the Father—that's God in Heaven—is through the Son. That's Jesus."

I turned to Will, who, in our couple of years as friends, had never said a word on this topic, pretty sure I'd gain an ally. "What's your take on this?"

"That's what I believe too," he said calmly.

"Whoa, really?"

"I believe Jesus is the son of God; he lived; he was crucified, died, and was buried; and then he appeared alive to hundreds of people a few days later. And it is through his death and resurrection that our sins can be forgiven. We don't behave a certain way to *earn* our way into heaven; that's impossible because we all fall short of that. We try to act a certain way because we are grateful for what Jesus did for us…because we know we can't *earn* our way in."

Silence.

Neil added, "Yep. Saved by grace through faith. Undeservedly saved from our sin because of Jesus."

How was it, I thought, *that in all the times Will and I had hung out at this point, he had never said anything about this?* This seemed like a pretty big thing to sit on and then unload on me in my room while studying for a sociology exam. I honestly don't remember how that conversation ended—probably awkwardly, given where I was on the topic at the time—but I would never forget the conversation, and hearing Mr. Hogan read Neil's name from Will's phone brought it all back.

*****

The coma week ended just as it had before, and the call from Alex was not much easier this time around. Again, this time I thought I could have—no, *should* have—done something more to save him. At the funeral, I still couldn't muster up the courage to speak.

I guess I will have to send Will's mom the card again with the words I planned to say. Or maybe it won't matter if this keeps happening.

And that's when I started to get hopeful. In *my* reality, as I started to call it in my own head, he had died three times and come back twice already.

What's to say it won't happen again?

Before I failed to speak (again), I stood in the hallway of the funeral home, waiting for the service to begin and watching people watch the slideshow video on the mounted screen. One of the older guests turned and said to another, "As tough as this is, I'm glad his organs were able to go to five different people. Such a blessing for them."

"Blessing?" I blurted out. A gathering of people turned to look my way.

Ann was one of them and came over to gently take me by the arm to guide me out of the funeral home and into the steamy summer blacktop parking lot.

"Honey..."

"What the hell? My best friend is lying in a coffin, wearing a damn baseball hat to hide how swollen his head still is, and this idiot has the nerve to say this is a blessing?"

"He meant for the recipients of Will's organ donation."

"I know, but that's bullshit. You make it sound like Will *decided* to make this donation. He was a healthy twenty-six-year-old man with his entire life in front of him. He was moving back home to be with his family." I was sobbing and clenching my jaw by this point. "He was a good person. He was everyone's best friend. How fair is that? To say this is a blessing is like saying it was right for God to take him. That's *not* the kind of God *I* want to know."

The words stung her; I could tell. I wish I hadn't said them, not because I didn't feel them, but because I didn't like hurting my newlywed bride. To her credit, she didn't say anything—she just held my hand while I took a few breaths and regained what was left of my sanity.

"Ann, I just can't see how this evens out. If anyone's going to call Will's death a blessing, those five people who got his organs better be freaking saints. They have no idea the pain their new body parts are causing so many people."

She let the words settle and then added, "I'm sure they're very grateful, even if they don't know the cost. Maybe you could try to meet one of them."

After her last comment, the thought of the organ donation recipients came back, as it had with Alex at Starbucks. It had still been more theoretical, like when you write a check for an organization where they can feed a kid in some faraway country for sixty-five cents per day. You know—or you hope—there is a real kid eating something somewhere as a result of your check, but that's about all you can do at that point. Even if they send you a picture, you think it could be the same stock kid photo every donor gets in the mail. For the first time, I started to think about the actual humans on the other side of this posthumous organ transaction.

Who are they? Where are they? Can I meet them if I want?

The rest of the afternoon went as expected, including carrying Will's casket into the vehicle, making the slow drive to the cemetery, and looking back—once again—at the miles of cars lined up to say their last goodbyes to the brother we lowered into the ground.

That night, lying in bed, reflecting on the day from hell I'd just lived a third time, I became obsessed with the five people who literally had pieces of my best friend in their respective bodies. If Will was gone and others lived on because of him, I had to know more.

The next morning, a Saturday, I dug in. Ann, having just completed nursing school after a stint in pharmaceutical sales, could tell me more about how it works with donor recipients, and the news was not good. Their identities—and the donor family's identity—are closely guarded in a sort of double-blind way. Neither side must ever meet the other unless both agree to meet, and that is all done through the agency that arranged the donation.

I was too uncomfortable about the whole thing to call Mr. and Mrs. Hogan. I wasn't sure how they'd react to a focus on those who *benefitted* from Will's death—still (and forever?) a raw, traumatic event, which might have blinded *all* of us to any possibility of *positive* externalities to come from it. But especially the two people who brought him into this world. So I started with Alex.

"Hey," he bluntly answered on the phone.

"Hey, how's it—never mind. Don't answer that," I caught myself. "I was calling with a thought—a proposal, I guess. Or maybe it's just a question."

"Okaaay?" He said, drawing out the end of the word and definitely ending in a question mark.

"So your parents were generous enough to sign off on having Will's organs donated to five different recipients. I've been thinking about these people a lot lately—like what their stories are, where they are from, and stuff. Any chance you and your family would want to meet them?"

"I don't know, man. It's a really tough time. I just…I just don't know."

"How do you feel about talking to your parents about it to see what they think?"

"Yeah, I mean, I guess I could."

"It may be good for us—I mean for them—for all of you to know who these people are, how they've been impacted, and everything."

"I'll talk to my mom about it. I'm sure there's a whole process of how to connect too."

I affirmed his belief and filled him in on what I'd learned. We signed off on the call and agreed to reconnect once he had a chance to talk to his family.

About a week later, Alex updated me on the conversations. His parents were not interested in meeting anyone. They were in too much pain and felt it would only slow their grieving process, not help it. Their act of generosity in signing the paperwork on that horrible June day would be the end of their engagement with Gift of Life. And who was I to question that decision? Alex's siblings sided with their parents, perhaps more to be in alignment with them and support them than to support their own desires. But I could be wrong. However, the good news was what the Hogans told Alex after sharing their decision. They would support his decision if he wanted to meet the organ recipients. It was not something *they* wanted, but they wouldn't stop him. In fact, they'd help facilitate for him any meetings he might want to pursue.

He wasn't sure what he wanted. Side with the rest of his family vs. follow my suggestion.

"Do you think you'd be more into doing it if I were to join you and be there to support you?"

After a contemplative moment, he responded, "Yeah, I suppose I would."

"Do you think your folks would be okay with me being a part of that?"

"I don't know for sure, but you know my mom loves you, RJ. I'm sure she'd be fine with it."

I raised my eyebrows and said, "Well, what do you think?"

He nodded and said, "I'll ask."

Two days later, he called me with confirmation and started the process. One week later, he called again with details of our first meeting, which would be a mere five miles from my condo in a city park. It was time to start to piece together the rest of the story.

*****

Alex and I pulled through the park entrance and made our way through the winding roads within the park until we reached the pavilion. As we pulled up, a couple appearing to be in their late thirties and two small children stood up from one of the picnic tables.

I turned to Alex. "You ready for this?"

"No." He paused, shrugged his shoulders, then reached for the door handle.

As we both got out of the car and started toward the family, the woman began wiping tears from her cheeks. The girl, about eight, and the boy, about five, held their parents' hands. The man—average height, good-looking with the beginnings of the George Clooney salt-and-pepper look—stared at us intensely in a way that showed that he didn't really know what else *to* do.

Extending his hand, Alex said, "Hi, I'm Alex Hogan, Will's brother."

The man's stare was broken, as was his composure. He took Alex's hand and pulled him close, embraced him, and began to cry softly.

"I'm Trevor Anderson," he said as they came apart from one another. "I have your brother's heart."

Both men wiped tears away in joy and sorrow. After hugs and introductions to me and Trevor's wife and kids, we settled into the picnic table they had been sitting at when we pulled up.

"So what's your...story?" I asked Trevor awkwardly.

He replied, "Well, um, I guess the short version. Kelly and I met in college and then moved around a little bit as I attended medical school, did my residency, and then a fellowship...I'm a pediatric surgeon now at St. Stephen's Hospital. Kelly works part-time in the library at the kids' school and volunteers as a tutor in an underserved community nearby. Emma here just finished second grade, and Owen recently graduated from kindergarten. They're both great kids and very active with karate, piano lessons, and soccer—just like their dad."

He smiled. As he spoke about them, he looked at them with pride, but there was also gratitude in his eyes—like the look an old friend gives you when he hasn't seen you in a while and the two of you are catching up at a reunion.

I was transfixed on the detail that he worked at the same hospital where Will died as he continued. "We've had quite a journey together as a family. Emma was born very prematurely while I was doing my surgery residency. She required four surgeries before she was six months old—a lot of complications, sleepless nights, NICU couch sleeping, and so on. We're very thankful that today she is an energetic soon-to-be third grader living a normal life...we weren't always sure that would be the case..." He trailed off, then snapped back into the moment.

"She's the reason I went on to do a fellowship in pediatric surgery. Seeing the impact those surgeries had on our family and the relief of our helplessness as new parents pulled me to provide the answers to families' prayers for *their* kids. So that's what I try to do now..." he added, trailing off a bit again. He and Kelly silently gestured to each other, and then Kelly encouraged the kids to go check out the playground structure. They ran off, likely happy to get away from boring adult conversation.

"Then, six months ago, I developed a virus—it didn't seem like much at first, but it progressed very quickly and moved into my heart, causing cardiomyopathy. I went from being a healthy forty-year-old to being on the transplant list in a matter of two weeks. From my hospital bed, we met with a lawyer to create my last will and testament, and we waited…not knowing how long we'd have to wait or how long I had *to* wait. There was a good chance I didn't have long… Now I've never been much of a spiritual person. After all, I'm a surgeon—I believe in science, evidence-based interventions for professionally diagnosed conditions, and excellent training and technique in the operating room. *That* is what I believe answers families' prayers."

Trevor now stared down at the picnic table under his folded hands.

"But, I will say, when staring death in the face and really believing I would surely die…well, I don't know where you guys stand on all this…I'll just say that I prayed to a hypothetical god…sort of a way of hedging my bet on science, or maybe a way of having a higher power *support* the science. I guess it was kind of a thing where, if there was no donor, there was nothing science could do for me. So I—we—prayed that if there was a god, that he…or she, or whatever…would somehow find me a heart. I made some deals during some quiet nights lying alone in that hospital bed."

He looked up now, right at Alex.

"And then we got the call."

This made Alex look down at that same nothing in particular on the wooden picnic table, knowing what that "call" was, why the call came, and likely feeling the same painful tinge I felt—bracing for what was to follow.

Trevor continued, "When they find an organ that is a match, everything moves quickly. I was prepped and in the operating room within hours. It was a long surgery but a smooth one. Of course, I was in no position to offer the surgeon any critique," he added with a wry smile. "From the phone call to seeing Kelly and the kids and my parents in the recovery room, it was ten hours…ten hours that was the answer to our prayers." He stopped abruptly, almost not completely saying the last word.

This was followed by uncomfortable silence from all of us. It might have been as strange for Trevor to say to us as it was for us to hear from him that the answer to their prayers was, well, Will's death. I thought about how competing prayers would work. It was a zero-sum game, after all. You don't get pediatric surgeon Dr. Trevor Anderson's miracle without Will Hogan's *lack* of a miracle. While I know they hadn't thought this way, when Trevor and Kelly prayed their hedging prayer to their hypothetical god, they were essentially praying for Will's car accident to occur, his lack of recovery after a week, for him to become brain dead, and for his heart to be healthy and saved—for all of that to happen exactly as it had. If not to Will, then it had to happen to *someone*. It had to happen, or Trevor was a goner. I looked out at Owen giggling and chasing Emma in a circle around the swing set. I'm sure you know what I was thinking, Dad.

Alex broke the silence. "Thank you."

"Thank *me*?" Trevor questioned.

"Yeah, thank you for meeting with us and telling your story. It…it's somehow both painful and relieving at the same time…I don't know how else to say that."

"I can only imagine," Trevor replied. "Thank *you*. Thank your parents for us. I know you said over email that they weren't ready for this kind of meeting. The decision they made gave me my life."

Tears flowed freely down Kelly's face, and, while she couldn't muster any sound, she nodded and mouthed the words "thank you."

They asked about Will and what kind of person he was. Alex and I shared stories of Will growing up playing baseball and lacrosse, his intense loyalty to his friends, his sense of humor, and his undying love of practical jokes. We talked about how many weddings he had stood up in by the age of twenty-six and how long the line of cars was at his funeral, but mostly we laughed.

When we both grew tired of sharing, Alex said, "Well, I guess that's it. We will let you guys enjoy the park as a family. Please keep in touch, though. This was good."

We all stood up and started to go in for handshakes and hugs when Trevor stopped us. "There is one other thing if you want." He nodded at Kelly, prompting her to reach into her purse.

"I brought my stethoscope. You don't have to, but if you want, you can listen to Will's heart." This stopped us both in our tracks. Alex looked at me, and I looked back at him wide-eyed. He reached out, and Kelly handed it to him.

Trevor helped him position the stethoscope properly, and Alex closed his eyes and softly cried while listening to his brother's beating heart in another man's chest. I took my turn. What a bizarre and moving experience. It was as if Will was alive again—or rather, *still*. I mean, if he had had functioning organs in five different people, including his *heart* of all things, then I supposed that in a way he *was* still alive—just not in the way *I* wanted him to be—and not in the way I'd *experienced* multiple times at that point.

Listening to Will's actual beating heart transported me to the heart he drew at our fraternity house in the spring of our junior year. As you remember, May was when my ex-girlfriend, Brandi, had just told me the week before that she was moving back home from Seattle and wanted to get back together. I was over-the-top excited, as I had never gotten over her in the two years since she left. It was her first night back in town, and after a long night of letting loose during our fraternity's house's annual Hawaiian Party, she and I were finally alone again in my second-floor room of the then-quieter post-party house. I will spare you my thoughts and intentions at that moment, Dad, but you can imagine that I was happy to have her home. But Will had other ideas. He still wanted to hang out and kept knocking on my locked bedroom door. At first, it was funny, and we told him to go away. It was really late, even by post-college fraternity-party standards, and literally no one was still wandering the halls drinking whiskey. No one except Will, that is. Anyone who knew him knew the only things that rivaled his loyal friendships were his need for hijinks and his persistence. He sat on the ratty hallway carpet with his drink in hand and knocked repeatedly on that door for *two hours*. He was definitely trying to stop me from having that time with Brandi, and eventually the laughing turned to annoyance.

"Dude, seriously—go to bed and leave us alone!"

"Nope. We need to hang out still. The night is young (hiccup), my friend."

"No, it's not. You are the only person still awake in this house."

"Not true. You are two and are too still awake...too," followed by his trademarked giggle and another hiccup.

"What the hell! Just go the F to sleep."

"Nope. The night is young, and you are young, and I am young, and we are going to drink more whiskey and hang out. There will be plenty of time for you, lovebirds, to reconnect. We are young, and I am young, and you are young, and the night...is young."

"No, it's not. *Please* leave."

"No, sir. No, sir. Not happening. We are young. I am young. I will always be here. I will always be young, and I'm not going away, so you're just going to have to deal with it and hang out with me."

And the knocking continued.

Eventually, Brandi and I decided that we weren't going to win this argument by convincing Will of anything. We also didn't want to stay awake any longer, and we certainly didn't need any more of Will's whiskey. We gave him the quiet treatment and just lay in bed, holding hands, happy to be back together. Will kept talking and knocking until he gave up. We thought he might have fallen asleep in the hall. Shortly after the knocking stopped, we fell asleep too. When we got up and drowsily headed downstairs the next morning, we found a four-foot by four-foot heart drawn on the living room carpeting in dish soap. I never even needed to ask who was responsible. I now wonder if something in Will knew that I shouldn't be with her, and I would later find my true love—a better match—and maybe he wanted to intervene to stop me. (As you know, Will would later play a role in me meeting Ann.)

Or, maybe, it was just the whiskey.

I returned from Will's soapy heart art to his beating heart in Dr. Anderson's chest. I slowly removed the stethoscope's earpieces and handed them back to him just as he said, "Your brother has a good heart. I listen to it every day."

Kelly, who had been very quiet, suddenly added, "You can too if you want." She reached into her purse and pulled out a thumb drive, handed it to a confused Alex, and explained, "I recorded your brother's beating heart for an hour while Trevor slept last night and saved it on this. You can listen to Will's heart anytime you want to be close to him, and when your parents are ready, they can hear him too, alive and well in my husband. There are no words I can say to properly…" She couldn't finish.

With that, there were no more words any of us could say. We hugged as Owen and Emma rushed back over, perhaps sensing playtime was over, and Alex and I walked back to my car, no tears left and weak in the knees.

We plopped down in the front seats, exhaled, and both stared straight ahead at nothing in particular.

*****

We were back on campus. I was walking across the street with Will and another fraternity brother from our Greek-lettered house toward the parking lot near the tennis courts. I looked at him, and it was as real as possible, but I knew he had already died. I told him I missed him and said it was so good to see him again. He stopped walking, prompting us all to stop. He looked at me as if trying to calm a crying baby, held his hand flat like he was going to give the ground a high five, then moved it in a sweeping upward motion to the sky, and said in a simple childlike way, "I go fast."

I woke up with my heart pounding. It was just before dawn, the morning after meeting Dr. Anderson and his family.

Man, that dream seemed so real.

I was with him again, and it was so real that it made me ache. My shaking from trying to contain my tears eventually woke Ann. She didn't even ask what it was about because she already knew that any time I randomly cried, it was because of a thought, a memory, or a dream about Will.

This was months after his (most recent) death, but everything felt so fresh, and I was on edge about whether my reality would repeat again or if this was it. This had now gone longer than the previous episodes, or whatever you'd call it. Every day, I hoped to see his number on my caller ID and see the beginning of another chance to save him for good. Little did I know how soon that chance would come.

At 11:30 that night, I was already asleep, and this time it started in the form of a 2004-style text message that read, "R u still up 4 Monday?" from Will Hogan. I quickly replied, "Y." My mind was so scattered. The lump in my throat was one-part excitement that I'd maybe get to see him again, one-part recognition of my grip on the real world slipping more and more through my fingers.

How long will this last?

I wasn't sure how much longer I could do this. I thought about how I couldn't just let him come home as planned and get into an accident. I looked around. I was on the air mattress on the floor in Northern Michigan again, back at the soccer tournament. The timing all made sense.

I texted back, "U take train?"

"N. parents SUV w. my stuff. moving. duh."

Right, I thought. I was unraveling to the point where I'd forgotten why he was coming to town. I had to think of a way to change his plans, though.

"Come tom not Sun" I typed.

"Cant. Stil have 2 pack more."

Texting wasn't working, so I called him. It was also great to hear his voice again.

He picked up on one ring. "Hey, hey. Everything all right?"

"Yes. I mean, it is now. You? You're okay?"

"Yeah, just about to go to bed. Gotta finish packing all my junk tomorrow for the move. Sorry if I woke you up—you seemed confused."

"Lately, I'm not sure what's going on. I mean…no, everything's good. I'm good. Hey, can I help you pack and drive back?"

"Um, I guess. Where are you?"

"In Petoskey for a soccer tournament."

"That's not exactly close to Chicago."

"It's also not much of a difference between me driving to Chicago versus me driving to Detroit. I'll leave in the morning, help you finish packing your stuff, and then maybe we can get a jump start and get you home on Saturday instead of Sunday. That way, you can be with your dad for *all* of Father's Day. It will be a nice surprise for him."

"Um, okay, yeah—I mean, I'm sure I could get everything done quicker with another set of hands. Thanks, man. Wait, what about the tournament? Isn't it, like, just starting tomorrow?"

"We had our first game tonight, with two scheduled for tomorrow. It's okay. I tweaked my knee a bit tonight, so I wasn't going to play tomorrow anyway," I lied.

"All right then. See you when you get here. What time you thinkin?"

"I'll leave early morning and get there around 11 or so."

"Cool, cool."

"See you soon, buddy."

"See ya."

*****

Driving along the west coast of Michigan, I drove in and out of good radio frequencies, and while scanning through channels to find anything other than country music, I was caught by a woman's smooth voice saying the words "their reality," so I stopped scanning. It was a radio interview on NPR with a psychiatrist who answered questions about schizophrenia, prompted by a news story about a mentally ill man injured by police during an altercation that started when the man stood shouting in the middle of a busy intersection.

"The hallucinations are most commonly auditory: hearing voices—sometimes familiar, other times strange or scary. Less commonly, the patient experiences visual hallucinations, which are, of course, seeing things or people that aren't really there. Particularly in the early stages of illness and sometimes *throughout* the illness, especially if left untreated. The patient does not recognize that these sounds, voices, or images are not real and are not seen or heard by anyone else." She stopped herself. "Let me clarify something I just said. When we say 'not real,' what we mean is that these things are not real to anyone *other than the patient*. For him or her, these things can be as real as anything else in their lives that others *do* see and hear."

The interviewer followed up with, "Earlier, you mentioned delusions as well. How are those different from hallucinations?"

"Yes," the professional, academic, yet soothing, made-for-NPR voice replied. "While hallucinations are auditory or visual, delusions refer to the patient's *thoughts*. These are often thoughts of grandeur—perhaps that the patient is a god, thoughts that everyone is plotting against him or her, or that the government is in some way out to get them or watch them. These are common clinical presentations. Additionally, patients may have delusions that involve control, which makes sense when you think about them losing control of reality. It is like the brain's way of trying to wrestle back some control. What I mean by control is that the patient will believe that he or she can control things, such as the outcome of a sporting event, when a traffic light turns green, or heroism like saving lives. Naturally, this goes hand-in-hand with the god-complex grandiose delusions. Finally, there are also common mood symptoms, such as depression, that accompany the other symptoms we've discussed."

"Thank you, Dr. Lyons. Is there anything else you feel our listeners should know?"

"Yes. We've come a long way in the last ten to twenty years in our understanding of this condition and in the ways it can be treated. The advance in medicine during this time has aided our ability to treat these patients in an outpatient setting. That is, we rarely hospitalize, or, as some would say, 'institutionalize' these patients for extended periods. While their level of function with treatment varies and is rarely what we would call 'high functioning,' these patients can now live meaningful lives in our communities. But it is very important for them to seek treatment, and often that is prompted by a family member or someone close."

"Thank you so much for your time with us this morning, Dr. Michelle Lyons."

"My pleasure."

I went back to scanning and quickly landed on a top forty station. The doctor's words settled on me like a blanket that grew heavier with each passing yellow line on the highway. For the first time, I cried, not for the loss of my best friend. I cried out of fear for *myself*.

*****

When Will opened the door to his apartment, I greeted him, not with the usual "bro hug" handshake/hug combo move that men do to avoid "too close" intimacy with another man, but with a two-armed tight squeeze that (again) must have lasted longer than comfortable. I hadn't seen him in several months…my time.

"Whoa, dude—you all right?" Will asked.

"Um, yeah—all good. Just a long drive, and good to see you," I replied, swallowing the peach pit in my throat.

"Yeah, you too. How's your knee?"

"What? Oh, um—it's okay…a little sore."

After we got through packing some of his bigger stuff into the SUV, we filled a small box with framed photos from his coffee table. As he placed Alex's family group shot into the box, he looked at it and said, "Now that Alex and Sarah have baby Eli, I'm just really looking forward to getting home…being around and doing stuff with them…being the fun uncle, you know? You know I'm going to be a bad influence on that kid." The last comment was followed by Will's signature eye twinkle.

All I could muster in response was a nod. I certainly hoped he would have the chance to be that fun uncle, and I was going to do everything in my power to help him do that, but I was beginning to question my ability to make that happen.

We loaded the last of the boxes and bags, and Will said, "All right—thanks again for helping me speed this up, so I can get back tonight. That was cool. You want to lead or follow?"

"I don't really know my way out of here and onto the highway as well as you do, so why don't you lead?"

"Makes sense. You gonna come to my parent's place or head straight back to your place?"

"I'll come say hi to your folks."

"Cool, cool." And then he got in his car.

*****

As Saturday afternoon gave way to Saturday evening, the sunshine we had had all day gave way to clouds seemingly chasing us from behind as we headed east toward Detroit. And as Illinois and Indiana highway signs gave way to Michigan's, those clouds caught us and began to let loose—nothing crazy, but enough of a spit to combine with the growing darkness to heighten my pulse. I hadn't even realized it rained in the area the night before Father's Day because I had been in Northern Michigan for the tournament. Driving along I-94 east of Jackson, the hair on my neck stood at attention. This was, of course, where his original—I mean, where Will's accident had taken place. Except now, it was perfect because the construction cones so familiar to Michigan drivers were still off to the right side of the road, not where they would apparently be the next day when construction would have one lane closed, leading to a slowdown that would take my best friend's life.

I relaxed my grip on the wheel a bit.

This is working.

Suddenly, two deer bounded out of the tree line to our right, about fifty yards ahead. Fifty yards is long when throwing a football, but not when driving seventy miles per hour through misty dusk. With Will leading, I screamed, "Nooooo!" as I slammed my foot on the brake. I skidded but didn't notice much about my own vehicle. My eyes locked on that tan SUV, swerving hard left to avoid the deer. It was too hard left. The weight of everything he was carrying home, the speed he was going, and how hard he yanked his steering wheel left to avoid the deer—it was all too much. The tank flipped on its passenger side and then rolled four times before screeching to a halt amid flying sparks.

What I saw has been seared into my amygdala for all time. The first time the vehicle struck the pavement on the driver's side, the window shattered. No window remained, and with each subsequent roll, it was Will's head that I faintly saw through the mist coming in and out of that open space, his body thrashing about just as his floor lamps, picture frames, and lacrosse stick blew out through every other window. I had heard descriptions of Will's accident "the first time" it happened, as told by the police-officer-turned-witness to his parents. I had heard about the rolling SUV and the head trauma that resulted. It was horrific to hear. It was a hundred times that to *see*.

I grabbed my flip phone from the cupholder and dialed 911 while I ran toward the wreckage. Another motorist, seeing me holding my phone to my ear, yelled that she had already called and was giving directions to the dispatcher, so I hung up just as I arrived at the battered metal load. The vehicle lay on its passenger side, with Will being held aloft by his seat belt, all of him hanging like a wet rag on that black strap. Dad, the blood, the pain. I just. It's so hard to even write about any of this.

My plan was supposed to work. It was working.

I just crouched on the pavement and shouted to Will that everything would be okay. I knew it wouldn't.

The ambulance arrived within some frame of time beyond my comprehension at the moment. As I raced after the ambulance to the hospital in Jackson, it occurred to me that in what I named in my head "the first accident," Will was taken by helicopter to Ann Arbor, and now we were heading in the opposite direction by ambulance. I wondered if he would get the same level of care this time around. I wondered if it would matter. But as soon as I wondered, I answered myself aloud with, "It won't." A new emotion bubbled up for the first time in this whole strange ordeal—*resignation*.

It was I who broke the horrific news to Mr. and Mrs. Hogan this time, not the police standing at their door. Over the phone, I had to describe the accident of their youngest born in as much detail as to communicate the gravity at hand and as little as to somehow soften the blow—as impossible as I knew that must be. After I hung up, I mentally checked out. I didn't remember the rest of the drive to the hospital or where I parked. I numbly watched myself hugging his parents and siblings from some place four feet above the action. Hours later, through a fog, I watched the organ donation representatives join the Hogans in the room and paperwork being signed.

Didn't that happen many days after the accident the first time? Now only hours?

That was it. He was gone again.

With the benefit of years of reflection, I now believe the slow-motion out-of-body fog I entered was simply human biology preserving and protecting itself from incomprehensible pain, like the way people black out and go into shock when they suffer a gruesome injury. The pain of his event and more rapid death was amplified by witnessing the whole thing and serving as a reporter to those who loved him most. I wished it all away. I wished I hadn't interfered because it made it worse. Well, worse for *me* at least. Will's conclusion was unchanged. As was the story for five others who benefited from that paperwork I watched getting signed in slow motion. For those five people, Will still answered their prayers with each pounding rotation his parents' packed SUV took on I-94.

The funeral.

The opening to speak I left unfilled.

The baseball hat.

Carrying the casket.

The traffic line at the cemetery.

I sank deep again. What were previously sobbing conversations with Ann about anger at God—if there was one—were now somber conversations dripping with my acceptance of everything around me.

I still wanted him back, though. And to be clear, I still felt strongly that I would have that chance.

*****

Shaving—slower than usual—in front of the mirror the day after again carrying the casket, I stared at the gray-blue eyes staring back at me.

Who am I really? Am I truly here? What is this? The psychiatrist on the radio—was she describing me? Was that interview even real? Have I lost reality? Am I creating my own? But this is different, right? She said schizophrenia sufferers experience a reality no one else shares with them, but everyone around me is living this alongside me. Those hugs with the Hogans at the hospital were real. There were seven other men hoisting that casket with me yesterday. We all shared those experiences. Just as they had the times before. Those were not voices in my head or images only I could see.

Is this going to last forever? Is this some sort of hell—experiencing your best friend's death over and over for eternity? How do I break this? Do I want *to break this if it means never seeing him again?*

Amid my distracted thinking, my razor blade went sideways like everything else in my life. Pinch. Slice. Blood quickly ran down from the base of my left sideburn.

That pain is real. I felt that.

I did it again, this time intentionally and on the *right* side. Pinch. Slice. Blood. Real pain. It dripped faster from both sides into the sink. I bowed my head as if to pray and studied the blemished sink. The pinch of the slices faded, but I focused on the sight of the warm blood blending with the white shaving cream to form two pink rivers meeting in the basin below. I chuckled. A Goo Goo Dolls lyric Will and I belted out in the car one day in college on the way to a football game popped into my head: *When everything feels like the movies, yeah, you bleed just to know you're alive.*

Well, I am alive, at least.

Allowing my mind to follow the memory of our purposely over-the-top performance of that song on the way to the Mitchel College football game led me to our chance encounter outside the stadium's main gate. Will trailed me as we headed for the gate when a too-thin midtwenties pale-skinned woman and her elementary-school-aged son seemed to light up when they saw me. Oddly enough, I didn't know them. Not surprisingly, it turned out they weren't lighting up for me; it was Will.

"Hey, Will!" the young brown-haired boy shouted as he gained a pep in his step and strode faster toward us.

"Hey, hey, Jessie," Will replied positively but understatedly. "Ms. Phillips, nice to see you. How are things?"

"We're all right. Thanks, Will." She glanced at me, and Will noticed.

"Oh, this is my friend, RJ. RJ, this is Ms. Phillips and her son, Jessie."

I was waiting for the rest of the story as to why—in the middle of this small college town where students rarely left the four-square-mile campus—Will seemingly knew these "townies" quite well.

"Nice to meet you both," was all I said.

Jessie looked up at Will with a smile and wide eyes as Ms. Phillips turned to him and said, "Thank you, Will. I know I don't get to say it enough because I'm not there when you pick Jessie up and drop him off with my mom, but thank you. He loves spending time with you, and it means so much to him. He thinks the world of you, isn't that right, Jessie?"

The boy, who couldn't have been older than seven, nodded embarrassingly.

"Aw, so now yer being shy! He was talking all last night about wanting to play lacrosse someday. He just loved playing catch with you on the *actual college field* with your equipment."

"Well, your son is a good listener and quick learner. He will make a great Mitchel College lacrosse player. I'm sure."

Will looked like he enjoyed being around Jessie, but he also wanted to keep moving into the game. He looked at me, to my left, at the game clock, counting down three minutes until kickoff, then turned back to the Phillips tandem.

"We better let you both find your seats and get to ours before kickoff…"

The thin woman agreed, "Oh, yeah, game's gonna start soon. It was so nice of the college to give us these tickets, and if you had something to do with that, I thank you for that too."

"Eh, it was nothing. Enjoy the game, you two. It was good to see you, Jessie. I'll see you Wednesday after school, okay?"

The boy nodded and obliged Will's outstretched palm with a high five before he and his mother headed toward their section. Will started toward the gate, and I followed.

Catching up to him, I asked, "Who *was* that?"

"Jessie is my little brother through the Big Brothers/Big Sisters program. We hang out every Wednesday."

"How did I never know you did this? I've never heard you mention it."

"Well, um, I guess I've always thought telling a bunch of people about it would make them think I'm doing it for that reason…to tell a bunch of people about it. Or to get women to like me or something. By keeping it to myself, I know I am doing it for the right reason—for Jessie. He's a good kid who's had a somewhat crappy life."

Here was my fun-loving, mischievous friend who I thought I knew everything about, and he was keeping a secret about himself doing something selfless and amazing, and the reason he kept the secret was that he didn't want people to think he was selfless and amazing. My mind was blown.

"That's pretty freakin' cool, man," was all my early twenties machismo would allow me to spit out in reply to this revelation. He turned to me, eyes twinkling in a way that told me he was trying to come up with a smart-ass remark to break up the mood, and just nodded his ballcapped head back a notch or two and pursed his lips in acknowledgment.

This memory of one of the best guys I'd ever known snapped me back to my mission: if given the opportunity again, this time I would make no mistake. Despite the pain, despite the horror of witnessing his accident, and despite my exhaustion, I *would* save Will.

*****

About a year prior to this, a local doctor, whom my friend Jamal knew as a customer, received a diagnosis of chronic lymphocytic leukemia and needed a bone marrow transplant. Jamal rallied everyone he knew locally to give a blood sample at a donor drive on a Saturday to determine if anyone would match the doctor as a possible donor. I was not a match. Sadly—if memory serves—no one else was either, and Jamal's customer died within the year.

Forty days after burying Will (for my most recent such occurrence), I received an email from the bone marrow donation registry organization. My heart beat a little faster when I opened the message, thinking about what this might mean. It turned out to be a generic mass email thanking those who remained in the registry and included a short success story vignette and a photo of a recent donation recipient. I locked in on the photo of a large dark-skinned man with a closely cropped jet-black beard, sitting on his porch step, smiling, with his elementary-school-age children and wife at his side. The caption below read, "Without people like you, Kevin wouldn't be here today." It transported me back to the city park with Alex, Dr. Anderson, and his family.

Without people like Will, Dr. Anderson wouldn't be here today.

I closed the email without deleting it, thoughtfully gazed blankly beyond my laptop at the large bookshelf in the corner of my home office, and eventually regained focus on the burnt orange spine of one book on the shelf; its all-lowercase title read: *the five people you meet in heaven.*

The five people.

While nearly six weeks had passed since Will's last death, I still held high hopes that I would have another chance to save him, and there *were* those five people out there somewhere. I had only met Dr. Anderson thus far—a remarkable story, to be sure. My back stiffened. I looked away from the bookshelf and back to my email inbox, then I picked up my phone and dialed.

I need to find purpose—if there is such a thing—in this pain.

"Hey, RJ, what's up?" the voice answered.

"Alex, what would you think about trying to meet Will's donor recipients?"

*****

The conversation with Alex was a familiar one. He shared how the process of donor families meeting organ recipients worked, the rest of his family's hesitation in meeting them, and his willingness to investigate it further and bring me along for support. It was the coffee shop conversation without the Starbucks noise.

Within a week, I received a call back from Alex. He had four names of those recipients who had agreed to meet.

"What about the fifth?" I pressed.

"Still waiting to find out about that one."

"Huh. Okay."

"But we've got four of them, with contact phone numbers and email addresses."

"I'm glad those four signed on for this. Are *you* up for this, buddy?"

He paused.

"I don't know. I guess let's try one and see how it goes. Do you care who we call first, or should we just go alphabetically, like they are on the list, and start with Anderson?"

"No," I responded way too eagerly, drawing a puzzled response.

"Whoa. Um, okay. Why?"

"Haha, I dunno. I guess having always been toward the end of the alphabet, I'm sensitive to that." Of course, I couldn't tell him we'd already *met* Dr. Trevor Anderson and that he had listened to Will's heart beating in the man's chest. In this new reality, he never experienced it. But I had, and I wanted to meet the others. "Maybe we could go in reverse alphabetical order."

"Okay, weirdo," Alex jabbed playfully, but also annoyed. "We'll do it your way. Let me call this Keith Young, and I'll let you know what's up with a possible meeting."

"Cool, cool."

There was silence on the other end for a moment, then Alex responded, "You sounded like Will just now."

"Sorry about that. I, uh, I didn't mean anything by it. I just heard him say that so many times. I guess it rubbed off on me, and talking to you brought it out."

"No, no worries." Alex's voice cracked a bit. "I'm just still really raw, ya know?"

"I know. I mean, I couldn't *possibly* know because he was your *brother*."

"Thanks, man. It's just…brutal."

We sat in silence, which would have been easier sitting together at the noisy coffee shop. It was broken when Alex's tone changed, and he offered a quite resolute, "All right. I'll let you know what Keith Young has to say."

"Sounds good. I'll talk to you then."

*****

He said yes to meeting with us. Meeting number two would happen for me. Two weekends later, I rode shotgun in Alex's Jeep Cherokee, heading south to meet fifty-four-year-old Keith Young in Norwalk, Ohio—a town of no more than about twenty thousand people after which, it turns out, the norovirus was named. It was also the birthplace of legendary football coach Paul Brown, a fact more likely to appear on signs around town than mentions of the virus. After quickly making our way through the small downtown that Mom would have likely called "cute," I referenced my printed MapQuest directions and told Alex to turn right toward the apartment complex address. We pulled up to the Walnut Creek Apartments, followed the winding roads, soon found unit 17E, and parked.

We walked past a rusty blue Ford Ranger pickup truck parked in a spot marked "17E." It was a piece of junk to be sure, but all in one piece, and it would likely get him from point A to point B. Alex found the intercom box and buzzed the worn white button under "Young— 17E." After several seconds, a raspy voice came through the speaker.

"Hello?"

"Hi, it's Alex Hogan, Will Hogan's brother. We emailed about—"

"I'll be down in a sec."

Alex and I exchanged looks, both no doubt wondering why we weren't buzzed in and invited up to 17E. He shrugged his shoulders, and we waited. Through the narrow window aside the teal external door, we saw a slightly green-skinned man appearing to be in his mid-sixties, lumbering down the stairs and turning toward us. He had shoulder length, thinning, very-dirty-blond hair, a graying blond mustache, and a spotty beard that hadn't decided between silver and blond just yet. His skin looked seventy. When he opened the door to greet us, we were first greeted with the stink of stale cigarettes.

"Keith Young," the shaky and raspy voice said as he extended his hand. We shook it and introduced ourselves. "My apartment's a mess. Why don't we go over to these benches this way?" he posited but had already started walking in that direction, so it was more of a statement than a question.

We followed Keith and his scent to a couple of iron benches with chipping green paint and followed his lead by sitting down.

Exhaling deeply and turning to us, he said, "So what would you like to know?" His voice came from the bottom of an ashtray, while also sounding like a man doing a bad impression of the late Katherine Hepburn, like his vocal cords had stage fright.

What would we like to know?

Taken aback, Alex spoke first. "Well, like I said in my email, my brother Will was a really special guy, and—" His voice cracked and stopped, so I took over.

"Mr. Young—"

"Keith!"

"Sure, sorry. Keith, we're just trying to put a name, a face, and maybe a story to the folks who received my friend Will's organs when he died. He was a great friend to many, and he was only twenty-six years old. We are going to miss him like crazy. We understand you now have his liver…"

"Yes."

Awkward silence.

The shaky voice continued, "Ya know, I'm not good with stuff like this—my ex says I don't express myself well. That's partly why she's my ex." He paused, cleared his throat with a guttural cough, and adjusted his thick glasses. "I'm sorry about your friend," and then looking to Alex, "about your brother."

"Thanks."

When it seemed like he wasn't going to say much more, I tried to move us along with, "Keith, would you mind sharing a bit about your story, a little about you, maybe why you ended up needing a liver?"

As uncomfortable as it seemed for him, he started, "Well, I s'pose I drank through the one I was born with. Another reason my ex is my ex, but the truth is she is a drinker too—just couldn't deal with mine no more. Course I'm sober now. Had to get sober to get on the transplant list. Course gettin' sober was also something the courts was wantin' from me for quite some time as well…"

"Oh, yeah?"

"Yeah, multiple DUIs will do that…So I'm doin' the best I can to not touch booze no more—ain't easy, but just trying to survive I s'pose." He took out a pack of cigarettes from his cargo shorts and offered one to each of us. We politely declined and told him we didn't smoke.

"Yeah, I had to quit to stay on the transplant list, but it's hard enough stayin' sober, so a guy's gotta have somethin', right?" Keith said, prompting him to laugh a little, which quickly turned into a cough and the hocking of a yellow-green phlegm ball the size of a quarter onto the ground to our left.

He adjusted his wire-rimmed glasses, wiped his mouth on the right sleeve of his white "All-Star Plumbing, Heating, and Cooling" T-shirt, and tried to compose himself enough to continue. As he did, I thought about how Will and I shared a mutual distain for people who drink and drive—a story for another time as to specifically why, beyond the obvious—and how this guy, Keith, who now had his liver, had had multiple DUIs. That thought, combined with the cigarette smoke exhaled near me, made me a little sick to my stomach.

"So that's pretty much the story, guys. I was a drunk. My wife and daughter left me years ago, and we don't talk much. I'm doin' my best every day to stay sober. I'm hoping that will help get me a better relationship with my daughter, at least. I work. I come back to my apartment to watch a little TV and grab some dinner, then I get up the next morning and do it again. I needed that liver to keep goin', and I'm gonna try to take good care of it best I can. Day I got the call from the Cleveland Clinic sayin' they found a good one for me was a great day. I'll never forget—gave me a shot at least at keepin' goin' and maybe fixin' some things."

That *liver?*
A good one?
A great day?

I could see Alex gripping his car keys in his pocket, so I stepped in.

"Thank you, Keith, for sharing your story with us. We will be sure to tell Mr. and Mrs. Hogan about you. I'm sure they will appreciate learning about the man who now has their son's liver."

"Okay. Be sure to thank them for me. I know they had to sign off on stuff to make the donation possible and everything. As I said, I don't have a good relationship with my daughter, but I can't imagine losing her, so I know it must be tough on them."

"You can never imagine," Alex replied coldly.

"Don't s'pose I can," answered Keith before standing up and extending his hand again. "It was nice to meet you both. Thanks for coming all this way. Thank you again for your brother's liver, and I'm sorry for your loss."

Alex blankly shook Keith's hand, as did I, and we thanked him one last time before turning toward the Jeep in stunned silence at the brevity of our reunion with Will's liver and its rough host. After each of us climbed into the SUV, we exchanged exhales and glances. He looked back at the steering wheel, gripped it tightly with his hands at "10 and 2," and slowly set his forehead against it. Tears quietly flowed down his cheeks and into his gritted teeth.

"This was a mistake," he muffled toward the dashboard.

"That was rough, I know."

My bland response was met with a moment when it seemed like he might compose himself and shake it off, but that moment soon gave way to an eruption through those tear-soaked, gritted teeth.

"*That* guy has my brother's liver! *That* guy? He doesn't deserve to have any *piece* of Will. He is a chain-smoking alcoholic whose family hates him, and *he* gets Will's liver? And the piece of crap is barely even appreciative. I mean, I heard him say 'thank you' but I didn't *feel* 'thank you.' He has no idea…no idea…no idea about the sacrifice it took for him to continue living his crappy life."

I tried to swallow the swelling in my throat as I sat with my own pain and shared Alex's.

He continued, "This was a mistake. There aren't five people out there," gesturing out the front windshield, "who will measure up to Will… Not even five of them *put together*."

A big part of me agreed. The other part of me knew Dr. Anderson's story.

"I agree, man. It's gonna be impossible to find five lives who can make up for Will's death. *Impossible*. But wouldn't you rather know *something* about them?"

"I don't know," Alex replied, staring out at the apartment complex. "I just don't know."

*****

It was a long and mostly quiet drive back to Detroit, which gave us both a chance to think. I knew if I suggested we meet Trevor Anderson next—going against my odd reverse alphabetical order request—Alex would have a very different experience than with Keith Young. But I worried that if, somehow, the meeting with Trevor didn't go like it did the first time or that Alex decided after meeting him that he didn't want or need to meet anyone else, I wouldn't have the chance to meet the others.

Do I recommend Trevor Anderson for Alex's sake or try to convince him to continue with the plan for my sake, knowing it might mean more pain and disappointment?

As Alex steered the Jeep up our detached condo's driveway, it was clear that the three-hour drive back was enough time for him to work through his thoughts, and my dilemma was solved for me.

Alex turned to me and said, "Thanks for going with me. I'm going to call Malcolm Reems. He's next on the list as we work our way up. I'll let you know what I hear about meeting up."

I nodded. "Sounds good. Thanks for letting me come to these meetings with you. That was rough today, but I just feel this need to meet these people."

"Yep. No problem. Call you this week sometime."

"Cool, cool."

Alex stared at me an extra tick, smirked, and shook his head as I climbed down out of the Jeep and headed inside to tell Ann about our day.

*****

The voice of reason demeanor I played for Alex gave way the moment I hugged my wife, and she asked how it went. Using some of Alex's apartment complex parking lot language, I unloaded my thoughts about the coarse Keith Young and the bleak future I forecasted for my best friend's liver and ended my diatribe with, "It just doesn't seem fair."

"Aren't you being a bit harsh, honey?"

"Ann, you weren't there," I snapped back.

"I know. He doesn't sound like someone we'd hang out with. He sounds like someone who has a lot of problems and has made a lot of mistakes in his life. So maybe him receiving this liver transplant is exactly what he'll need to turn things around. Maybe he'll fix things like he said he was going to try to do. Maybe God's plan for him is beyond our understanding."

"God? Yeah, I'm still not ready for that at this point. If God's plan for Keith Young just *had* to involve flipping Will's SUV over and over and bashing his head against the pavement through the shattered window, I'm not sure that's a God I'm ready to worship."

With that, I sobbed from the anguish I felt, and for the ache I knew I caused Ann with my comments. She didn't deserve any of this. Being who she is, though, she just wrapped her arms around my neck and pulled me in closer to her, my chest heaving.

"I'm sorry," I offered.

At that, she held me tighter.

Nothing else was said about it for the rest of the night. We watched some dumb TV show on the couch and got ready for bed and the beginning of another work week—another week of wandering around the planet, trying to relate to others who didn't recognize what I was going through, trying to wrap my arms around the neck of reality and sanity and hold on tightly before they slipped away from me for good.

*****

On Thursday night of that week, my cell phone caller ID read "Alex Hogan."

"Yo," I answered.

"Hey, buddy, how's it going?"

"I'm okay. Just another week, ya know? You?"

"Same here. It took some back and forth, but I got in touch with Malcolm Reems, the next person up on the list. He agreed to meet us if you're still in."

"Absolutely, let's do it. When and where?"

"Saturday in Indianapolis. You sure all this is okay with your newlywed wife?"

"Yeah, she knows I'm going through a rough time, and she's been cool about all of this crazy stuff I've been saying and doing. I can drive this time. What time do you want me to pick you up?"

"Lunch with Mr. Reems is at one o'clock, so how about eight?"

"Sound good. '*Mr. Reems*,' huh?"

"Yeah, the dude sounded really old over the phone."

"Old, huh? What, um, donation did he receive?"

"Eyes."

"Eyes?"

"Yep. I didn't know that was a thing, but I guess it is."

"Hmmm. Well, I guess we'll just have to *see* how this goes."

Simultaneously, Alex over the phone and Ann from the kitchen groaned, and I could feel their eyes rolling at my bad joke—one of my qualities of which I am most proud.

*****

My Pontiac pulled up Alex's driveway three miles from our condo at exactly eight o'clock on Saturday, and his wife waved to me from the front door as he ambled toward me with coffee and donuts in hand.

"Hey, thanks for driving."

"No problem."

"Are you trying to grow a beard?" Alex asked, trying to suppress a smile.

"I don't know. Just haven't been shaving this week, I guess."

"You know, Will would have been able to grow a better beard in nine hours than you've managed this whole week."

"I know. No one can compete with your brother in hair growth. I might as well not even try."

Alex laughed. "Dude, shave it. It looks bad."

"It turns out there's no such thing as an eye transplant." I changed the topic as we got onto the highway.

"Huh? Why would this guy tell me this over the phone?"

"I asked Ann about it last night when we were discussing this road trip. You can't transplant an entire eye. No such thing. He may have said that, but what he likely meant was a cornea transplant. It's the front part of the eye that helps you focus light, so you can see."

"Well, okay, then. Good to have a wife in medicine, huh?"

"Comes in handy quite often."

The remainder of our four-plus-hour drive to the Indianapolis suburb of Lawrence was a mix of quiet contemplation and chatter about whether the Tigers were ever going to get better. (Who would have thought in 2004 that they would be in the World Series two years later?)

With Alex giving me directions from the printed MapQuest sheets in his lap, I pulled the car through the middle-class neighborhood until we reached a clean white bungalow at the end of a cul-de-sac. The elderly black man who sat on the porch in a folding chair waved to us as soon as it became clear that we were turning into his driveway. He turned, opened the front door, hollered something inside, then slowly got up and carefully made his way down the front steps to greet us as we opened the Pontiac's forest-green doors. The shine of his white teeth against the backdrop of his wrinkled dark skin was likely seen for blocks.

"Welcome to Lawrence, gentlemen!" the man said enthusiastically.

I slowed my walk to allow Alex to take the lead. He started with, "Thank you. It's good to be here. Alex Hogan," as he extended his hand.

"Malcolm Reems," the man said, extending his right hand while the left held steady to a cane. As I introduced myself and shook his free hand, three other people came out the front door. "It's so nice to meet you both. Let me introduce you to my family." They all dutifully lined up for their patriarch's introductions.

"This is my son, Ronald." The middle-aged man's handshake was as firm as his father's, and his goatee was the same white color as the elder's head. Ronald then introduced his energetic wife, LaSonja—with her enthusiasm for our visit seemingly springing forth from her dark, tightly curled hair, which was pulled back in a bun—and their shy, tall, dark-skinned, teenage daughter Kameron. After all handshakes were exchanged, which LaSonja upgraded to loving hugs, Malcolm suggested we head to the backyard where there was some shade. He heard no arguments from me, as I was already sweating from a couple of minutes out of the air-conditioned car. We slowly followed him step-by-step up the driveway toward the fenced-in rear grassy space and followed his lead by sitting in the chairs around the patio table. LaSonja brought lemonade and snacks out for all of us.

"So…" started Alex, clearly trying to think of a way to start a tough conversation.

"So thank you," interjected Malcolm. "And I am so very sorry about your brother. I know I have no words to properly express it. But thank you from my entire family."

Based on our meeting with Keith Young, this direct and appreciative utterance took us both by surprise.

"Thank you for saying that," Alex responded with a nod.

Malcolm continued, "I had five brothers who were all very special to me. Four of them have passed. Martin died way too young, and I still feel that pain today. I think about what he could have done…" As he trailed off, he looked at shy Kameron and added, "What he could have *had*. So while I can't say I know *exactly* how you feel because I don't know you and I didn't know your brother, I have *some* idea. And I wouldn't wish upon anyone what you must have gone through these last many weeks, but I just want you to know that I am appreciative. I thank you. My family thanks you from the bottom of our hearts."

Alex and I were in tears. We felt the love of all four of them. We felt it for Will. We shared a bit about his twenty-six years of life, about his sense of humor, his character, and the love he had for his family and friends. I shared that I would always remember the last glimpse I had of him in the casket, wearing his high school baseball hat.

"He was a baseball player, huh?" Malcolm joined in.

"Yes, sir."

"I played baseball a very long time ago too," Malcolm responded, looking at Ronald, who nodded as if to give approval for Malcolm to continue with what the two men knew he wanted to say. "I'm not shy enough to avoid telling you fellas that I was a good player. I was a professional player first in the Negro American League—I played for the Indianapolis Clowns from 1950 to 1953. Can you believe that was the actual name of the team? Anyhow, that was only a few years after Jackie Robinson became the first Black player in the Major Leagues, and change didn't come as fast as we would have liked. In 1951, I had a teammate with the Clowns for three months who you may have heard of—a guy by the name of Hank Aaron." One side of his lip curled into a grin as he paused for effect, having just name-dropped one of the greatest players to ever play the game. Ronald had the smile of a man who had heard the cadence of this story many times before.

"Of course, he was only there for three months because he was too good not to be scooped up by one of the big clubs, which he was, by the team then known as the Boston Braves."

Another pause.

"He went from a Clown to a Brave."

After a pause for a sip of lemonade, which LaSonja had already dutifully refilled, he continued, as if reading from a script. "My chance came when I was picked up by the Detroit Tigers in the winter of '53. They had me start with their AA team in Little Rock, where I did very well and found my way up with the AAA Buffalo Bisons, where I was good enough to stay and try to earn my chance to get called up to the big club. I came close many times, and then in the fall of '56, I got the phone call of a lifetime. I was a second baseman, and they had injuries at that position, so I got my chance. I spent two weeks with the Tigers, got into a half dozen games, and went three-for-fifteen from the plate. That's batting .250 over two weeks in Major League Baseball. Not bad. But not good enough. Got sent back down and never got another call of a lifetime. One more hit per week over two weeks would have put me at five-for-fifteen—that's batting .333, and I probably stay—or at least get invited back some time. Baseball is a game of inches, boys." These words seeped with the pain of regret. "After two more full seasons in the minor leagues in Charleston, making no money, seeing no hope for a future in the majors, and finding out I had a son on the way, I hung up my cleats for good and got a job making Jeeps in Toledo, Ohio.

"It was a good life. I worked hard, retired, and moved back to Indy to be closer to the fine folks sitting with us at this table, shortly after Ronald's job brought them here. It certainly hasn't been a stress-free life, but I have been blessed. And then...my vision started to go out on me..." He tailed off and took a moment to collect himself.

"I had once been able to see the stitches on a curve ball, and there I was, not being able to see worth a darn. They call it Fuchs dystrophy. It started when I woke up in the mornings with some fuzziness, and then as the day got going, everything was fine. I just thought my eyes were getting a little tired with my advancing age. Then that morning fuzziness got longer and longer throughout the day. After more doctors' visits than I can count and worsening over a few years, I was considered legally blind. Can you imagine that? From seeing the stitches on a curve ball to being legally blind. Hardest part was having my sweet Kameron go from a beautiful baby to a fuzzy child to an invisible teenager." His eyes welled up as he relived the time.

"After getting the cornea transplant surgery...after getting your brother Will's corneas, I could see my family again. I could see Kameron crystal clear for the first time in years. And as you boys can see, my sweet Kameron was a beautiful sight indeed."

Kameron smiled bashfully and looked down at her lemonade.

Malcolm continued, "Ronald's mother and I didn't see eye to eye on everything." He paused, perhaps realizing the irony of his phrasing. "We split up many years ago. She then had a stroke twenty years ago and passed. So this is us. This is my world right here," he said, motioning to Ronald, LaSonja, and Kameron holding their lemonades around the glass patio table.

Alex awakened from the trance brought on by the remarkable story we'd just heard. "I'd say you have a great world, Mr. Reems. Thank you for hosting us today."

"Oh, it is all *our* pleasure. Thank you, boys, for coming down. And thank you...for everything," Malcolm said as he looked around the table at his everything.

Malcolm nodded, then reached across the table for Kameron. Placing his hand on hers, he whispered loudly enough for all to hear, "Honey, would you play your violin for us?"

"Oh, grandpa, I dunno." She looked at her mom, who only needed to display gentle eyes and a firm nod to let her know this request was something she expected her to fulfill.

Kameron reluctantly took her dad's car keys to the driveway to fetch the instrument out of the back of their Explorer. She returned, removed the violin and bow, looked at her nodding grandfather, took a breath, and played notes I'd heard many times before—most memorably by way of bagpipes at a Scottish festival near Mitchel College's campus. After beautifully—almost hauntingly—filling the backyard with the first few lines of music, Kameron's instrument was joined quietly by the voice of her mother, then her father and grandfather joined too.

I once was lost, but now am found
Was blind but now I see

The eyes beneath her jet-black bangs closed.

T'was grace that taught my heart to fear
And grace, my fears relieved
How precious did that grace appear
The hour I first believed

Her long, thin fingers shook from side to side as she pressed the neck of the instrument.

Through many dangers, toils and snares
We have already come
T'was grace that brought us safe thus far
And grace will lead us home
And grace will lead us home

The strings wept and whined out high-pitched notes.

Amazing grace, how sweet the sound
That saved a wretch like me
I once was lost but now am found
Was blind but now I see

Malcolm turned away from his granddaughter, looking directly at Alex.

Was blind, but now I see

Have you ever had tears stream down your face without weeping, and you're not even sure why? I hadn't until then.

I used my sleeve to wipe my face, and we quietly applauded Kameron's performance while she gently packed up her instrument, not anxious to continue with other songs, despite her breathtaking display. After another hour of storytelling and snacks, Alex and I thanked each member of the Reems family. Hugs and tears were exchanged, and we hit the road to head back to Detroit.

The long drive found us recounting the life story of Malcolm Reems and feeling thankful he and his family met with us. To be clear, it didn't make Alex and me miss Will any less or be any less angry he was taken from us, but it did feel good to see this man living a better life—one he seemingly deserved.

Because two men can't talk for five straight hours, the ride also found us in long stretches of quiet and personal contemplation. As we got closer to home, we passed through an intersection as the light turned yellow. Without a thought, I kissed the first two fingers on my right hand and touched my car's ceiling.

Alex said, "Why did you just do that?"

"Do what?"

"That thing where you just touched the ceiling."

"Oh, ha. I don't even realize I'm doing it anymore. A friend of mine in high school used to do that when she first got her driver's license, and I'd see her doing it when we drove around. It was her 'thank you' to the universe, or whatever, for the light being yellow and her making it through it before it turned red. I just adopted it as my own at some point and kept doing it."

Alex shook his head. "The only other person I've seen do that is Will."

"Yep, another weird connection we had. The first time I saw him do it, I thought maybe he'd seen me do it and was making fun of me or something. I called him out on it, but he said he and a high school girlfriend started it, and he just kept doing it. Kind of the same thing—a shout-out to the 'traffic light gods' for the yellow, not red, light. Although, as you know, sometimes those lights are, as my dad would say, 'pink', when we kiss the ceiling. We both couldn't believe someone else did this. So when we'd hang out and drive around, it was the only time either of us had someone else doing that thing in the front seat of the car with us."

"Weird."

"Yeah, I've still never met anyone else who does that. It was a silly thing, and I think I've done it somewhat unconsciously for many years now. Moving forward, it may take on a new meaning for me."

Silence.

When I dropped him off, he told me he'd let me know if any of the others agreed on meeting specifics. With that, it was back to his life of family and work, trying to hold it together while the rest of the world moved on. For me, it was back to trying to be present with my wife, pretending to care about my job, and preparing for Will to come back.

*****

For whatever reason, around that time, I started smoking. I mostly hated it (physically), but did it anyway, in some sort of self-harm, "we're all gonna die anyway, screw the world" move. Never around Ann, of course, though I'm sure I wasn't as good at hiding it as I would have liked to think. I coughed through them at first, but it made me feel connected to Will. He wasn't what I would call a "smoker." But he smoked. Does that make sense? He smoked when he drank, in rotation with a wad of Kodiak ("the bear," as he called it) in his lip when he wasn't drinking—sometimes on a long car ride to help pass the time. It was often a social thing—no surprise given that one of his many nicknames was "social lubricant."

The only time I ever tried the bear was because of Will. And the only time I had ever smoked a (portion of a) cigarette? Yep, Will too.

The chew was on a fraternity dare/bet/pledging secrecy thing we were sworn to protect with our lives. The short (and allowable) version of the story: I agreed to put one in my lip for ten minutes to help our chances of pledging being a little easier. Will supplied the "lipper." I stuck it in there for ten minutes, then I puked a few minutes later while walking to the fraternity house for that night's fun and games. Never again.

The cigarette wasn't a dare or bet; it was me making fun of Will. Shortly after college graduation, we sat outside tents at a Cedar Point campsite the night before a group of four of us were to hit the park's rides. While splitting a case of beer, Will and another friend smoked, and I made fun of how stupid they looked and how moronic it was that educated guys would ever smoke, even "socially." I can't recall how that led to me asking for one and lighting it up. I attempted to smoke it, looking as ridiculous as I could—not difficult. I coughed, choked, and put it out in the dewy grass. It would be great if that story ended there. Two weeks later, I had my new hire onboarding telephone call with the Human Resources department—what would now be an online survey to fill out was a telephone interview back then. There was a long series of questions—even what my shirt and ring sizes were. We talked so long, the interviewer, Joan, and I sort of hit it off; we had a friendly banter going. One of the questions about ten minutes into the discussion was whether I had smoked a cigarette within the past twelve months. I laughed.

"Yeah, I smoked one a couple weeks ago as a joke to make fun of my friends for smoking."

"Okay, so I'll put you down as a smoker then."

"Wait, what? No! I hate cigarettes. Like I said, I was making fun of them for smoking."

"I'm sorry, sir. If you've smoked any cigarettes at all in the last twelve months, I have to put you down as a smoker for your insurance information."

"Oh, no. Really? There isn't anything you can do based on the way I just described that to you?"

"I'm sorry. I'm just doing my job, and I don't want to get in trouble for lying. You can call the HR service phone line a year from now when you've been smoke-free for a year, and they will change it for you."

I was so pissed, knowing this would mean a higher health insurance rate, given that they would consider me a smoker just like every chain smoker out there. As I answered the other questions, I couldn't wait to hang up and call Will. He would cry, laugh, and destroy me over this.

She continued her questioning, and two minutes later, she asked, "When you travel for work, should I put you down for a smoking hotel room then, or a nonsmoking room?"

Sigh. "A nonsmoking room, please."

Will had a field day with it and found ways to remind me of my HR smoking status frequently over the next twelve months. So maybe after he was gone (again), I choked those smokes down to attempt to reconnect with him, yearning for him to be back and make fun of me again, or to try to become a little more like him—as if that would make him stay with us. Who knows? One thing was certain: I did not call HR to inform them of my new status.

*****

That Friday morning, I awoke to a phone call and jumped when I saw "Hogan" on the caller ID. It was Alex, not Will.

I should really change the way I have their numbers stored on my phone.

"Hey, what's up?" I grunted.

"Looks like we've got another donor meeting if you're up for it tomorrow."

"Absolutely. Where are we heading this time?"

"Middle of nowhere, mid-Michigan," Alex quipped.

"Sounds lovely. At least we don't have to leave the state this time. What do you know about the person we're meeting?"

"Young woman in her twenties who got Will's kidney—Gabriella Dominguez."

"Whoa. I didn't know people in their twenties ever needed new kidneys."

"Yeah, me neither. I guess that's a thing. We shall see."

"Okay, then. Your turn to drive. What time you pickin' me up?"

"Okay, princess," he playfully shot back. "Be ready a little before ten. They are hosting us for lunch in a park at noon, and it's two hours away."

"Cool, cool."

Pause.

"You really gotta stop saying that. You sound just like my brother."

"Sorry, man. I'm not doing it on purpose."

"All right. See you tomorrow morning."

To this day, I am grateful for Ann's patience with me during this time. We'd only just gotten married, and I was leaving for full days with very little notice and—despite my best efforts—was sometimes mentally nonexistent even when I was home with her. When she found me crying in my home office or in bed in the morning after one of my Will dreams, she usually just hugged me and listened if I cared to speak. She also continued to recommend that maybe I "talk to someone" (a therapist). I politely declined. At that point, I wasn't sure if these donor meetings *were* therapy for me or were only going to make the grief process worse. Either way, the next morning we'd head to the farm country of mid-Michigan to meet the carrier of Will's kidney.

*****

When I walked out to Alex's vehicle that morning, the first words he spoke were, "Dude, what is up with the growth?"—an obvious reference to my facial hair.

"Ah, yeah, I haven't shaved in a bit."

"In a *bit?*" He chuckled. "You and I both know that sorry excuse for a beard took you over two weeks to grow, and it still looks spotty as heck. Aren't you supposed to be clean-shaven for your job?"

"I don't care."

"Alright. Well, good try anyway," Alex jabbed, ready to move on.

"Sorry, I can't grow one in one day like Will."

"Is *that* what this is about? The way you're saying 'cool, cool,' the fact that I know you started smoking, trying to grow a beard—are you trying to become Will or something?"

I was uncomfortable. Someone else was seeing my grip slipping.

"I just…I don't know what I'm doing. I'm trying to hold on to him any way I can," I replied in a cracked voice, swallowing hard the pit in my throat. "I'm trying to save him…somehow."

"What are you talking about—*saving* him?"

"Sorry. I didn't mean that. I was just trying to remember him, I guess. I don't know."

Without saying much else, we both dropped the topic and spent most of the remainder of the drive silently listening to music. After two hours of nondescript farm country driving, broken up by several one stoplight towns, Alex steered his Jeep into the town of St. Louis, where we were greeted by a sign proudly declaring our entrance into the "Middle of the Mitten."

"This isn't middle of nowhere, mid-Michigan. It's middle of the mitten, Michigan," I ribbed Alex.

He shook his head. "I stand corrected."

Other signs told us of the population of only a few thousand and that former Detroit Tigers World Series champion Jim Northrup was a hometown hero. Other than that, it was a quiet town with a prison and the Pine River running through it. That river ran along the banks of the city park, into which Alex next turned. After a short winding dirt road past a baseball field, we saw the tired-looking wooden pavilion, where more than twenty people gathered and balloons were adorned.

"Is…is this for us?" I asked. "Are we in the right spot?"

"I don't know, man. I followed the directions they emailed. They didn't say anything about a big party or anything."

Alex parked, and we tepidly stepped out onto the dirt and gravel. At once, the eyes of the entire pavilion party turned to us while an olive-skinned man in his late fifties took the hand of a twenty-something woman who wore a floral-print blouse, a black choker necklace, and milk chocolate-colored hair. The pair walked toward us—her with a smile filling her round face and him with tears in his eyes—as we approached the pavilion.

She spoke first. "Are you Alex Hogan?"

"Yes. Are you Gabriella Dominguez?"

"I am. You can call me Gabi. This is my father, Edwin."

Alex shook the man's hand and expressed the pleasure of meeting him, while the man nodded politely and said in heavily accented English, "Hello and thank you."

"And this is my friend, RJ. He was a very good friend of my brother."

More handshakes, head nods, and warm, yet stilted, smiles were exchanged. Gabi and Edwin led us back to the packed pavilion, where food preparations had halted upon our arrival. As we approached the covering, Gabi spoke.

"Todos, estes es el hermano de Will, Alex, y su amigo RJ. Es a Will a quien temenos que agradecer por mi riñón."

The gathering erupted in applause and shouts of *"Gracias!"* and *"Alabado sea Dios!"* We were introduced to many people in rapid succession as they all came toward us. It was hard to keep them all straight, but as far as I can now remember, we met Gabi's mom, Irma, and her two older brothers, three pairs of aunts and uncles, and numerous cousins ranging in age from about twelve to thirty. Lastly, we met Edwin's parents, Edgar and Marta. The younger the family members were, the better their English (including Gabi's accentless speech). For the others, I did my best to keep up with my three years of mediocre high school Spanish as my only guide. We didn't need to know any language to understand the tears, hugs, and firm handshakes during those first few minutes at the park. Appreciation and love are understood without words.

Before we could find a place to sit, plates and utensils were thrust into our hands, and an authentic celebratory buffet was laid out across two picnic tables. Edwin and Irma insisted we get our food first ("Please, you go.") Once we had filled our plates, we were joined by Gabi, Edwin, Irma, and Gabi's brother, Ernesto ("Ernie") at one of the tables. Between bites of delicious stuffed peppers, spicy chicken, and flan, we answered questions about Will, and Gabi shared her story.

"My family immigrated here from Guatemala to work in the fields when I was three, so I don't really remember much of that time.

I am the youngest of four. You met my brothers. My sister had to work today, but she should be here in a little bit. My dad, his brothers, and my aunts work hard to support all of us and give us a better life than what they had when they were younger. That gave me the opportunity to do well in school and become the first person in my family to attend college."

I said, "Congratulations. Where did you go?"

"I am still a student at Central Michigan University. At twenty-four, I am one of the older students on campus, but that's because I missed two years when I got sick."

"Sick?"

"During the second semester of my first year at CMU, I got an infection that got so bad I ended up in the ICU for a couple weeks. The doctors told my parents I was lucky to survive. The problem was that the infection caused what is called acute tubular necrosis. I'm told it is rare for someone my age, so I got unlucky with that. It is a condition that shuts the kidneys down, and it wasn't found until my kidneys were very damaged. I had to be on dialysis, which meant trips to the clinic three times a week for four hours and taking a pause from my college career. And it meant going on the transplant list and my family and I praying for the miracle of a new kidney."

Irma spoke to Gabi, *"Diles lo enferma que te sentiste."*

"My mom wants me to tell you how sick I felt. That was a difficult time physically. As my kidneys got worse, I would get sick, throw up, and feel really weak. Just prior to the transplant operation, I was even starting to get confused. Things were not looking good."

While holding back tears, Edwin added, *"Pensamos que podríamos perder a nuestra niña."*

"My dad says they thought they would lose me."

Putting her arm around Gabi, Irma quietly added, *"Y luego nuestras oraciones fueron respondidas."*

Gabi hesitated to translate, and I didn't understand much of it, so I asked, "What did she say?"

"It is hard for me to say to you both because I'm afraid to offend or hurt you."

Alex responded, "Don't worry, Gabi. You can tell us anything."

"Okay... She said, 'our prayers were answered.' I hope you know she doesn't mean offense by that. It must be difficult for you to hear someone say that, given your brother's death."

Alex nodded. "It is difficult, but I know she didn't mean anything by it. Tell her I need her to teach me how to pray so my prayers can be more effective."

Gabi hesitated again, clearly feeling uncomfortable, but Alex gave an affirming smile, so she said to her mom, *"Necesita que le enseñe a orar para que sus oraciones sean más eficaces."*

We all exchanged uncomfortable smiles and silence and were glad when the crunching gravel from an approaching vehicle broke up the weirdness in the air. Once parked, a woman who could have been Gabi's twin got out, wearing a plain gray short-sleeve shirt with black piping, along with a black knee-length skirt and plain black shoes.

As she approached our table within the pavilion, I cheerfully greeted her, "Hello, Alma."

She gave me a puzzled look, then glanced down to find that she was still wearing her nametag from the local diner. "Oh my gosh," she said as she quickly unpinned it and stashed it into the pocket of her skirt.

Gabi laughed. "Alex and RJ, this is my sister...Alma, as you already know."

"I love your name," I added. "Based on my limited Spanish knowledge, I believe it means 'soul,' right?"

"That's right," she replied, her face turning another shade of red with the attention she was now getting.

Gabi added, "Alex's brother Will was the donor of my kidney."

As Alma shared her condolences for Alex's loss and joined the conversation about Will and Gabi's world renally intersecting, I couldn't help but drift a bit, thinking about her name tag and how I called her by name when she showed up. That was such a Will thing to do.

As you know, Will came from the upper part of the upper middle class. The son of two lawyers, he did not exactly want for much, and he was likely the only person in my circle of college friends who did not receive much or any financial aid to attend Mitchel College, one of the most expensive institutions of higher learning in the Midwest, as you well know, Dad. (Thank you once again to you and Mom for finding a way to make it work.) However, Will was also the only person I knew at Mitchel who worked at Jim's Snack Shack on the western edge of campus. While the rest of us handed over our student IDs to have meal plan money deducted for our 10:00 p.m. fried mozzarella sticks study break munchies, he wore a hairnet and dropped those sticks into the fryer. I don't even know why. I don't know if there was a backstory about how spending money was earned in the Hogan house, if he was in trouble for something at home, or if Will just *chose* to work there.

I *can* tell you he wore a cheap pinned name tag on his purple school-color apron and that he made it look cool—not because he *actually* looked cool (because he didn't), but because he didn't *care* that he didn't look cool. There was something so next-level about his spirit and his ability to be comfortable with who he was and what he was doing at any point in time, completely free from worries about judgment. In fact, it was like he was *daring* someone to judge him. Maybe that's why he worked at Jim's. But I remember that name tag the most because, long before I read Dale Carnegie's *How to Win Friends and Influence People*, I learned about the value of using people's names from Will Hogan. He called everyone by their names. *Everyone.*

We'd be at a bar, and he'd find out the bartender's name right away and use it all night.

The parking attendant at a concert. "Thanks for your help tonight, Jerome. Be safe out here."

The lady buckling your seatbelt on the amusement park roller coaster. "Thanks—have a good one, Debbie."

I'll be honest: at first, I thought he was doing it ironically. To be a smart-ass. But the longer I knew him and the more time we spent in these different scenarios, the more I realized this was genuine, and the more I learned about how people repaid his small gesture with favors:

maybe that extra drink at the bar on the house or the preferred parking spot at the concert. I don't think that was his *goal*, though; it was just a by-product of the way he treated people. I once saw him pick up a dirty used coffee cup that fell into our walking path while a custodian removed the trash bag from its metal container outside one of the larger lecture halls on campus. He put it in the bag. The older gentleman bowed his head a bit and embarrassingly muttered, "Thank you." Will leaned to his right to see the worker's nametag on his all-blue jumper.

"Dennis. That's my uncle's name. I'm Will. You ever go by Denny?"

"Uh, oh, me? I, ah, yeah. My grandparents called me that when I was a kid."

"Well, the name suits you well. You mind if I call you Denny?"

The janitor paused, perhaps contemplating what sort of long-term relationship he would have with this twenty-one-year-old college student at the private college where he picked up trash in the evenings and mopped the floors.

"Sure. I guess that would be fine."

"Cool, cool. Have a good night, Denny."

"Yeah, okay. You too."

Other students wondered how everyone on that campus seemed to know Will and generally adore him. I didn't wonder. When everyone wondered why he gave a shout-out ("Denny!") from across the central outdoor mall and the janitor tipped his cap or gave a wave, I knowingly smiled. He accomplished this presence one dirty coffee cup at a time.

My daydreaming about Will and college janitors was broken abruptly when Gabi looked down for an instant and jumped up from her picnic table seat. At first startled, everyone quickly laughed when they realized what had scared Gabi was one of her younger cousins' toy snakes he'd thrown onto the ground next to our table. Like any good sister, Alma let her have it.

"Oh, my goodness, Gabi. You and this new snake thing. It is crazy, girl."

Surprisingly, her mom seemed to jump onboard the teasing as well.

"Pregúntale a estos chicos sobre el miedo a las serpientes."

Gabi and Alma both shook their heads and laughed.

"Mamá, no." I didn't have any trouble understanding Gabi's response.

After a few rapid-fire Spanish retorts, Gabi relented.

"Okay, you guys, my mom won't let this go. I thought this may be some old country Guatemalan wives' tale or something, but then I did find some websites that seemed to support the idea, so here it goes: Was Will afraid of snakes?"

I looked to Alex immediately because, upon a quick search through every memory I had of my best friend, I couldn't recall a single time where we were around a snake. Or even saw a movie with a snake. Nothing. It didn't take Alex long, though.

"Yes. He was absolutely scared of snakes. He could stare down a wild dog and seem totally chill with it, but he freaked out about snakes. Our one set of grandparents lived in the country, and he always avoided going deep back into their property because we would see snakes back there all the time. I think one really freaked him out when he was little, and he never really got past it."

Gabi and Alma and their father exchanged looks with the matriarch, who only needed to hear the word "yes" to brandish the motherly "I told you so" look.

Alex, a bit confused, tried to move the conversation along. "What a funny coincidence that you're also afraid of snakes, but I guess that is somewhat common. I am not a huge fan either, just not as extreme as my brother was." His last statement must have brought imagery to mind that made him smile, surely thinking of times he took advantage of Will's phobia, much to his younger brother's detriment.

Meanwhile, I sat thinking, *Weird. How did I never uncover that in all our years of hanging out?*

Gabi replied, "Well, that's what makes this so strange. I have *never* been afraid of snakes. I have worked in fields since I was small and would find them, pick them up, and wave them around—no problem.

My parents had to stop me from eating worms when I was small. But ever since receiving my new kidney—Will's kidney—I have been terrified of snakes. My mom swore to me that this was a part of my organ donor's personality coming into me. I just thought she was being silly, but I finally searched and found some websites that discussed a type of therapy called neuro-emotional technique based on the idea that emotions, including fear and even forgotten-about trauma, can be stored in different parts of our bodies, not just our brains."

Irma smiled and drew a unanimous laugh when, in beautiful, choppy English, she said, "Mommy always right."

"That is just plain weird to think a kidney could carry a fear of snakes," Alex contemplated aloud.

"I thought so too," replied Gabi. "But I'm finding it easier and easier to believe every day. I am majoring in psychology, and I'm even thinking now about pursuing research in this field. Seems I'd have a lot to offer, given my own personal experience. After today, I don't see how I *couldn't* follow this path now."

"That's amazing," was all I managed to add.

"This will give your new song *extra* meaning," Alma suggested to her sister.

"Song?"

"Yes, I'm in a band at Central. We do mostly covers, but I write sometimes too. I wrote a song called 'Gut Feel' based on this experience, but I wrote it without really *knowing* if this fear came from the transplant. My bandmates are gonna *freak* when they hear this."

The following hour or so included more eating than was comfortable and more trying to keep up with the conversation, armed with only those three years of high school Spanish classes. And of course, hugs, tears, goodbyes, and commitments to stay in contact.

During the two-hour drive home, my thoughts bounced from an immigrant American dream story almost cut short due to a freak illness, to a kidney that's apparently afraid of snakes, to wondering what kind of music Gabi's band plays and what "Gut Feel" would sound like. I pictured her as the lead singer on stage in front of a bunch of drunk college students, belting out emotional lyrics—

and so few people around her understanding their full meaning. I thought, *I should figure out when they're playing, and Will and I can go check them out.*

That happened a lot—innocently forgetting he's gone. See a funny movie and start to call him to tell him about it. Think about going to the bar with him to watch a big game, then having to change plans. Music was especially tough because we went to many concerts together, big and small. In fact, Dad, I'm not sure whether you ever heard the full story of how Ann and I met and how attending a concert with Will played a part.

The part of the story everyone knew was that Ann and I both worked in sales for competing pharmaceutical companies and were introduced by one of our mutual doctor customers. Well, it was actually his wife/office manager who was adamant we *must* meet. Ann and I had very different territories, only overlapping on one small zip code, where the city met the suburbs, and therefore only competitively "sharing" two medical practices. It happened that one of these two had a doctor and his wife—Dr. Faraz Mansour and Fatima Mansour—who took a liking to each of us separately and noted that we should no longer be separate from each other.

After months of them trying to convince me ("RJ, you will *love* her," Fatima said) to go on a blind date with this other sales representative, who sold a direct competitor medication nonetheless, and me trying not to mix business and pleasure, I finally relented. Due to scheduling conflicts, we spoke on the phone for two weeks prior to going on this blind date, increasing in call frequency as the date got closer. By the time we met face-to-face on March 29, 2002, it didn't feel like a blind date; it felt like we were already friends—like we knew each other already. After dinner at Lilly's Seafood in Royal Oak and seeing *Panic Room* at the movie theater, I dropped her off at her place with a hug and a peck on the lips. I could have floated home rather than driving. I could have proposed to her that night; I kid you not, the thought crossed my mind.

The next day, Saturday, I called Will to confirm our evening plans to see a friend-of-a-friend's band play at a bar on the east side.

He was still good to go. I told him about my date the prior night, and he could tell how into her I was.

"You should invite her to come tonight," he suggested.

"You don't think that would come across as too strong? Didn't I hear somewhere that you're supposed to wait a few days before you call a girl again, so you don't seem too desperate?"

"Dude, forget that junk. It sounds like you had a great time, and you've already been talking to her for weeks. Tell her there's a group of us going, and she can bring a friend, so she doesn't freak out about it."

"Ah, I see what you're doing," I jabbed. "You're looking for her to bring a cute friend *for you*."

"Hey, hey, hey," he quickly retorted. "Can you blame me?"

We both laughed.

I asked, and she said yes. She even brought her cute roommate. Much to Will's dismay, the cute roommate also brought her fiancé. After the half-hour drive to the bar, the five of us met my friend, whose friend was the lead singer (and freestyle beatboxer, as it turned out) of the friend-of-a-friend's band, and settled in with a drink at the high-top tables in anticipation for the show. Ann's roommate and her fiancé went to look for food menus, leaving Ann and I on our second date and first with Will. He started the conversation over the house music.

"So I've been thinking," he said, looking at Ann. "We've met before, right? I mean, we know each other somehow, right?"

Oh no, did they make out at some party somewhere? Please don't tell me this will be an awkward second—and final—date.

"I've been thinking the same thing," Ann replied. "Is your last name Hogan?"

"Yeah."

"That's how we know each other. In high school, I dated your brother Alex's best friend, Adam. We used to hang out at your house sometimes."

"That's right! Oh, man, it is a small freakin' world, isn't it?"

"It sure is," I jumped in, happy they had seemingly never had a relationship with each other that would make things weird or end this date. There was a pause, then Will continued.

"But we've seen each other more recently, haven't we?"

Oh no, here we go.

"Yep," Ann said cheerfully. "One night a couple of years ago, some friends and I were on our way to a coney place after leaving a club, and my crazy friend Veronica flagged you and some of your friends down while driving along Crooks Road and yelled that you should come with us."

"That's right! We ended up getting a table all together at the diner." Will let the remembrance sink in, then paused and turned to me. "RJ, you were *there*."

I *was*.

I get chills to this day when I realize our first date dinner at Lilly's wasn't the first time we shared a meal together. Two years prior, we had shared a table with our friends, eating greasy food at about two in the morning, and then parted ways. It took Dr. and Mrs. Mansour to bring us back together. Perhaps we both had some things we needed to do on our own for those couple of years before the timing was right for us.

So Will was with me the first time I met Ann. And with me again on our second real date, which he convinced me to set up the day after the first. We saw each other every day after that until she had to go out of town for work three weeks later. Three months after that, we talked about getting married. One year after that, we were engaged. One year later, we were married. One month after that, Will died.

True story.

*****

Some weeks later—forgive my lack of clarity; time became a strange and nonlinear measurement for me during this whole ordeal, as I'm sure you've gathered by now—Alex called again.

I really need to change that caller ID. I jump every time I see "Hogan."

"Hey, I've got good news and crappy news," was how he started the call.

"Uh, oh, what?"

"Well, the good news is I've got another meeting set up for us, the recipient of Will's heart, actually. Three weeks from Sunday. So that makes four of the five of them. The crappy news is that the recipient of Will's pancreas doesn't want to meet."

"Humph."

"Right? Ungrateful SOB…or B."

"Yeah, really crappy that he or she wouldn't want to meet us. Any idea why?"

"Nope. The agency that connects donor families with donor recipients doesn't give reasons. They just say whether each side will meet or not."

"That sucks."

"Yep…so anyway, nothing we can do about it. The other guy, with the heart, emailed me, and we're gonna meet up in a few weeks if you're up for another one."

"Absolutely," I said a bit more excitedly than usual, given my knowledge of Dr. Anderson and his family.

"Okay. I'll talk to you again as we get closer to the date."

"Cool, coo—sorry," having caught myself. "Sounds good. Talk to you later."

"See ya."

After we hung up, I hung on to the words I'd just heard, trying to wrap my head around how someone could receive a presumably life-saving pancreas transplant from someone he or she—in my head I assumed it was a man, for no good reason—doesn't know and does not have the decency to agree to meet the family of the donor whose death was the sacrifice needed to receive that pancreas. It was like Alex said—ungrateful. I just couldn't imagine being in his skin and thinking that way.

What scenario in his life now would have made that an okay decision? Didn't he realize the pain endured by those around this stranger, whose death was his saving act? He couldn't trouble himself to spend an hour to at least say thank you? Who even knows this guy, and what is he about?

SAVING WILL

This tore me up, Dad. I couldn't shake it. This guy (?) I'd never met seemingly devalued the life and death of my best friend. It ate at me for days. Then, another dream.

Dreams are, of course, often hard to explain, even when we do manage to *remember* them. This one was really tough. I was sitting at a picnic table at the small beach park near Ann's parents' house. There were several unknown people sitting around the table. Though I sat with them, I sat above them a bit, so I looked down on them. Across from me sat Will. But I wasn't really me. (Like I said, dreams are tough.) I was *Jesus*.

There wasn't a mirror there to see what I looked like or anything, and no one called me by name, so there was nothing in the dream to *tell* me that I was Jesus. I just *was*, and I somehow *knew* I was. And I was looking (slightly down) at Will, and we spoke to each other, but we didn't speak words. As we communicated and I looked at him, I felt warm—not sweaty like from the heat—warm *throughout*. And, most importantly, I knew Will and the other faceless beings around the table. When I say I *knew* them, I don't mean in the way that we currently know anyone in a human way. It was, in a way, so much deeper and all-encompassing that I couldn't even say what it was. I knew Will and the rest of them better than they knew themselves—better than anyone *could* possibly know *anything*.

That was it. That was the whole dream. It might have lasted for fifteen seconds, though who's to say with dream time? I woke up immediately after, which should go without saying because I remember my dreams only when I quickly wake up and take mental note of them. After this one, I lay in bed frozen, wondering what it meant. Perhaps it was just a way of coping, but after several contemplative minutes flat on my back, I landed on this: I would likely never know the pancreas guy, but he was known. He was known better than he knew himself, and he was loved so intensely as to create physical warmth. And so was Will.

*****

The succeeding three weeks leading to our meeting with Dr. Anderson and family (yes, *again*, for me) were relatively nondescript. I worked, ate three meals a day, and watched dumb reality TV shows on the couch with Ann. It felt routine. Months had passed since Will's (most recent) funeral. The pedestrian feel of life left me considering that Will might never come back and I'd likely never have another chance to save him, which got me down at times but was nothing close to where I *had* been. I still wanted him back, but an emotional toll had been taken. I was tired and slowly growing a bit numb.

The day before our scheduled Sunday meeting with the Andersons, I lay on the couch late in the afternoon, with Ann having met up with her mom for lunch. I still hadn't been sleeping well and continued having crazy dreams when I *did* manage a few hours per night, so the movie on the TV I'd seen twice already couldn't keep me awake. Saturday afternoon couch naps were some of the best sleeping I did anyway.

I don't know how long I was out, but I was awoken with a start by my cell phone's violent ring.

Dang, I should have turned off the ringer.

I caught a glimpse of "Hogan" on the caller ID before I answered.

I keep forgetting to change that, so I don't freak out every time Alex calls me.

I sleepily blurted into the flip phone, "Hey, what's up? We still on for tomorrow?"

"Well, hello to you too. I thought we agreed on Monday."

"Huh? Did they have to change it?"

"Wakey, wakey, dude. Hey, my bad for waking you up. Tomorrow's Father's Day, and I don't think that would be a great look for me to move back home and then ditch my dad on Father's Day, but I am looking forward to getting back and having a beer with you on Monday."

I snapped wide awake, pulled the Nokia away from my ear, and looked again at the caller ID with my heart suddenly pounding.

Will Hogan.

"Will! Oh, my gosh, I thought I'd never—"

What do I even say?

"Everything all right, RJ?" my best friend's voice replied with genuine concern.

"Yes. I just can't even tell you. I'm just so happy you're back. I mean coming back. I'm happy you're coming back home, Will."

"Me too, buddy. It will be good to be back closer to my family and friends, for sure. You sure you're okay?"

"I'm great, man. I wish I could tell you—it just took me a minute to wake up when you called, I guess," I answered. Only then did I realize that I lay on an air mattress on the floor of a living room in Petoskey; it was, of course, the Saturday morning of the soccer tournament.

"All right. Anyway, where do you want to meet up on Monday after work?" Will continued.

"Gelston Bar at nine?"

"Works for me."

There was a natural pause in the conversation. Gabi's face flashed into my head, and I pushed her away.

I must *save Will. Although everyone around me is experiencing the same reality, I am the only one conscious of its repetition. I am the only one who knows he's going to die. I am the only one who can save him. Everyone is counting on me without even realizing it.*

"Hey, what time are you leaving tomorrow?"

"I don't know exactly. Depends on how much packing I can get done the rest of the day today, but I'm hoping to be on the road by ten or eleven at the latest, so I can be back in time for Father's Day dinner at my folks' place. Why?"

Think, RJ. Think. What can I tell him? How can I change this?

I just uttered back, "Leave earlier if you can."

"Um, okay. What's up?"

"Nothing. I just know how much your parents miss you. I was, um, talking to them the other day, and they are super-excited to have you moving back, so you should surprise them and show up for lunch instead. You know how much your dad loves surprises."

"Good point. He does. You know him well. I'll see what I can do with the packing, like I said, and see if I can hit the road a little earlier."

"Great. I just know they'll love the surprise."

"Cool, cool."

"Okay, I'll let you go to do the packing, then. I'm really glad you called. Can't wait for Monday night."

"Likewise, dude. Have a good rest of your weekend and tell your dad tomorrow I said, 'Happy Father's Day.'"

"Will do. Drive carefully."

"Yep. See ya."

"Bye."

He was back again! I had another chance. If he left earlier, perhaps he would miss the end of weekend traffic returning from cottages to the Detroit area and make it through that construction zone unharmed. It hadn't worked before. Not when he went early alone or when I drove behind him and witnessed the horror for myself. But I didn't know what else to do. How else could I fix this mistake of a situation? What I did know was how hard it was to end that phone call. When he died, I just wished I could hear his voice again. I wished I could pick up the phone and call him to talk about—well, *anything*. Now I had had that chance again and again, even getting to see him again and again. But I was on edge, not knowing how or when I'd have these chances again. I was wondering how *this* time would be different.

How much longer can this go on?

We played two soccer games that day, and I remember nothing about either of them. I know we didn't do enough to earn our way into Sunday's final, which didn't bother me. I was only focused on how Sunday would transpire. I took it easy Saturday night at the bar and drove home early on Sunday. Ann and I hung out a little, and I turned on the US Open coverage.

The phone call from Mrs. Hogan sunk me before I picked up.

"Hello," I tepidly answered, bracing for the words I'd come to know too well.

"Hey, RJ, I just wanted to call to thank you for the nice surprise," a cheerful voice replied. "Will is currently in our kitchen making a Father's Day lunch for us, and he said it was your idea for him to get his stuff packed last night so he could make it back early to be with us. That was very sweet of you to encourage him like that, and Mr. Hogan and I want to say thank you."

In the background, I heard the normally demurred Mr. Hogan enthusiastically yell, "Thanks, RJ!"

I exhaled into the receiver (do you still call it that on a cell phone?) so loudly she must have thought I'd momentarily encountered a wind tunnel.

"Oh, yeah, no problem, Mrs. H. I just thought it would be nice."

I choked back excitement this time rather than tears.

"Well, it *was* nice. And please tell your dad we said, 'Happy Father's Day.' We hope to see you soon and more often now that Will is back home. We miss *you* too."

"Absolutely. You'll see me a ton, I promise. Tell Mr. Hogan I said Happy Father's Day, and tell Will I will see him tomorrow night."

"Will do, RJ. Take care."

It worked!

After hanging up, Ann was confused by the elation caused by me finding out my friend came home a few hours earlier than expected to make lunch for his parents. Talk about perspective. I did my best to explain it away, but something wasn't sitting right with her, so I continued talking, which led to me pulling back the curtain—a touch of reality.

"Ann, do you ever question what's real?"

"Huh?"

"Yeah, like, I know if you reach out and grab my hand right now, it seems real. I see your hand. I feel your hand. Maybe I smell your perfume. But how do I *know* it's real?"

"Were you watching *The Matrix* again?"

"Well, yes, actually. Great movie. But that's not what this is about."

"Well, then what *is* this about?"

"Have you ever seen, heard, or *experienced* something that *no one* else experiences the same way you do? Or, like, at all? Like, no one else would even believe you if you told them?"

"You're scaring me a bit with this talk. Are you okay?"

"I don't know. I just—I've had a really rough time lately... understanding what I'm experiencing."

"RJ, is this about our marriage? I thought everything was going well, and it's only been a few weeks."

"Oh, my gosh, no! No, no, no. It has *nothing* to do with you." I took her by the hand—saw her thin hand, felt it, and even smelled her vanilla-scented hand lotion. "I love you so much, and I love being married to you—forever. I don't know what I would have done without you during these last..."

"During what, honey?"

"I can't say. I've lost Will over and over again."

"Will? Like you've lost your friendship with him?"

"No, not that. I dunno. Maybe just forget it. I'm just happy he's moving back closer to us."

"Yeah, honey. We all are. But I'm worried about you. You can tell me what's going on."

We sat in silence for several moments.

If I can't tell her, who can I tell?

"Will died, Ann." My tears and each word poured out from the crack in the dam I'd built over many months of my repeated time. "It was so sad. I was *broken*. But you were awesome and so supportive. And then he was back, like it never happened. It never happened for anyone but me. And then he died again, and it was even more brutal. And this *keeps* happening. It keeps repeating, and I keep trying to save him, but I *can't*."

My speech got more rapid as I continued.

"He just keeps dying. It is so painful, and I can't figure out how to make it stop. I want him back, but I also want him to stop dying. It's just too much. And there are others. Other people he's helped. I don't know how to deal with them in all of this. But he's back now, and I have to keep him safe. I must save him *for real* this time. I don't want to go through this again. I have to make it stop. Make it stop! Make it stop!"

I couldn't speak anymore because I cried so hard I couldn't gather the breath to make more words.

SAVING WILL

Ann brought me closer and held me. It debilitated me to speak about these things, but it also made me feel lighter to get this out into the world for someone else—especially for the love of my life. Once I caught my breath, we pulled away from each other, and Ann quietly spoke.

"RJ, I think you need to get help. I think you need to talk to someone. These things you're saying…are…consistent with a serious mental health situation, and you need to see someone."

"That's why I didn't want to say anything. I know what I'm saying is not believable, but that doesn't mean it isn't *real*. It is so very real. Trust me—I wish it wasn't. I don't want it to be real."

"Honey, when people have psychotic episodes, it seems very real to them," she replied as patiently as she always does. "That's what this sounds like to me."

"I know. That's what the doctor on the radio said when I was on my way to Chicago to save Will. That's not me," I said forcefully, and I stood up and backed away from Ann.

"I'm not judging you. I'm helping you the best I can based on my medical knowledge. I love you, and I don't want to see you get hurt."

"I *am* hurt. I am *hurting*. But I don't know how a doctor could change that. I am the only one who can change this, and the only way to change this is for me to save Will. No doctor has proven they can save him yet, and I'm the only one who understands what's happening."

"RJ, would it be okay if I set you up to talk to a professional about all of this *while* you work out whatever you need to with Will?"

Silence.

"Whatever. Sure."

"Okay, honey. I love you, and I'm concerned for you. For us. I think this is an important step. I'm glad you shared these things with me. It's important to talk about this stuff."

And with that, we stopped talking about it, both doing that thing people do when a TV is on during a conversation that has hit a lull—casually titrating from communicating to watching. In this case, it was the US Open, which Ann couldn't have cared less about and on which I could have placed a surefire wager at the beginning of the day. She'd wait until Monday to find me help, and I'd wait until Monday to see my best friend alive once again.

*****

I glided through my workday with vim as I prepared for that night's reunion at Gelston Bar, mentally rehearsing what I'd say and do repeatedly throughout the day. At dinner with Ann, she informed me that I'd have an appointment the following day with a psychiatrist she'd heard good things about from a nursing school friend of hers. I agreed to make the subject go away. It was fine that I'd talk to someone, but I was hyperfocused on the task at hand, and that appointment had zero impact on my mission.

I got to the bar early and tensely waited for Will, breathing a sigh of relief while feeling a jolt of adrenaline when he sauntered through the front door. As before, we exchanged the usual "bro hug," which I held for an extra few beats.

"Easy there, big fella," Will joked. "It hasn't been *that* long."

"It's just…good to see you," was all I said again (despite my day's rather productive mental dialogue rehearsals), again fighting back tears, and grateful to again have this chance.

He plopped down into the booth I'd nabbed twenty minutes before and quipped, "Married life has made you a softy already, I see. You didn't tell me how Aruba was."

"Aruba?"

"Um, yeah, your honeymoon?" he replied, chuckling. "That memorable, huh?"

Aruba seemed like a lifetime ago. In my repeating realities, I didn't get to redo my wedding day and my honeymoon, though that would have been nice, so it didn't occur to me that our honeymoon was only a few weeks before this conversation in his timeline.

"Of course," I said with a forced snicker. "It was great. In the ten days we were there, we did a half-day snorkeling trip, a full-day jeep tour, and then a whole lot of nothing but sitting on the beach and by the pool and drinking fruity island drinks. So it was basically the perfect vacation."

"Cool, cool. Glad you guys had fun."

"Yeah, man, it was great."

"Dude, your wedding was such a fun party."

We again recollected the day and laughed about many stories, including Sam walking out of the reception hall carrying enough "last call" drinks to last until breakfast. I laughed at all the right parts of the conversation, as if I hadn't already had this conversation with him, and I was so thankful to hear the laugh he gave when his shoulders shook up and down and he coughed for air.

That is the laugh I am going to save.

He again talked about how he would miss Chicago but how happy he was to get home to Detroit, where his parents and three siblings all lived. He was especially happy to get to spend more time with his baby nephew—Alex's son.

Much of this was a repeat from our previous Gelston Bar reunion, but I changed its course with a new discourse.

"You sound like you're in a good place right now," I offered.

He seemed taken aback by the heavier-than-normal-dude-speak comment.

"Yeah, man. I'd say I am in a very good place right now," he answered before pausing, then continued, "I've been gone a few years since we graduated, you know. Colorado, then Chicago. It will be good to get back. I don't think I shared with you that Alex and I had a falling out last year."

I shook my head. It was the first I knew of it.

"Yeah. Some stuff was said that can't be taken back—from both of us. I won't get into the details. Just crappy stuff for brothers to say. It got bad enough that I wasn't sure if I'd ever want to come back closer to him and my family."

"Man, I had no idea," I said as we paused to allow the server to place the beers we'd ordered minutes before onto the table. "You said you're in a good place now, though?"

"Yep, it's all good, buddy," he said almost cheerfully.

"What changed?"

"Life is too damn short, dude."

Truer words were never spoken, especially considering the source.

"So that's it, then? You guys just decided to let it go?"

"Well, what I've learned is that no two people in a fight ever decide at the same time to not be in a fight anymore. It takes one person to make a move to start the process."

"Makes sense. Who made the move?"

"Me," he replied with a mixture of pride and contriteness.

"Good for you, Will. What got you to that point?"

He paused. His eyebrows raised as he sipped his stout. "I don't know if you really want to get into all of this with me again."

"Huh? Again?"

"Yeah. Do you remember our conversation with Neil Whitaker in the dorms that one night?"

Of course, I did. I'd been reminded of it when Mr. Hogan read through the contacts in Will's phone as he lay in a coma.

"Yep."

"It's on that note, if you are okay with me getting into it."

"Okay."

"So I was really struggling with this thing with Alex. I mean, he is my big brother, best friend, and mentor. All that. But I was really pissed, and I had already decided he was in the wrong. I am sure he feels the same about me." He paused and, with a sly grin, added, "Of course, he'd be wrong."

I laughed.

He continued, "Anyway, I was ready to just be done with him and stay out of town away from him to avoid the whole thing. One Sunday, I realized I hadn't been to church since I left Michigan. I guess I just hadn't shopped around in Denver or Chicago to find a place to go. So I showed up to an old stone church with ivy growing up its sides. I'd walked past it a bunch of times late at night. It was big, beautiful, and intimidating, but I felt drawn to walk through those huge double doors and find a seat on one of the back rows of wooden pews.

"The organ music and choir and all that was fine—I mean, beautiful for sure, just not my cup of tea. Before the pastor preached his sermon, a woman read a verse of scripture, and it stopped me in my tracks. It was from the Book of Matthew, where Peter says to Jesus, 'Lord, how often will my brother sin against me, and I forgive him? As many as seven times?' Jesus says to him, 'I do not say to you seven times, but *seventy times seven.*' I was meant to be there that day, RJ. I was meant to hear that. During the sermon, the pastor also quoted from Paul's letter to the church in Ephesus, something like, 'Forgive one another, as you are forgiven through Christ.' It really grounded me and shook me loose from this grudge I held. Here I was, not forgiving someone else—someone I love—for a wrongdoing against me, while I have been forgiven for my sins, of which there are many, through Christ's death on the cross. So I realized, or rather, I was *reminded*—who am *I* to refuse to forgive? So that was that. I called him from the front steps of the church, apologized, and forgave him."

"What did he say?"

"Well, we both ended up crying over the phone, and he forgave me. We both apologized, and there's been no looking back since. That's the big reason I wanted to move back home. I don't want to waste another moment being away from my family—being away from my nephew. I want to be an awesome uncle to him. I don't want to kill any more life, holding grudges with people. I'm turning that page and focusing on loving them."

"Wow."

"Yeah, wow, huh?"

We both nodded and sipped our drinks.

"Will, you have a lot to live for," I started while trying to craft my next phrasing. "I just want you to be careful. I mean, be safe and stay out of harm's way, you know?"

"Haha. Okay, I'll do my best. What the heck are you talking about, dude?"

"I, um, worry about you. You are a great friend, brother, uncle, and son, and I don't want anything to happen to you, so I want you to be careful. I don't know how else to…I don't want to lose…I dunno, man. Just take care of yourself is all I'm trying to say."

"Um, yeah," he said before adding his signature grin. He asked, "Do you know something I don't?"

All I could do was force a fake laugh, shake my head, and take the final sip of my ale. The dam was close to breaking again, but I held it in. After Ann's reaction, I didn't think there'd be any good to come from laying my reality on Will. I thought it would likely be an even more disturbing conversation given that it was about *him* dying. And he would probably freak out about still hanging out with me. He would have thought I needed to be in a padded room somewhere or something. I had already made things weird in the conversation, and that was clear in the way he broke our silence.

"Well, I'm already tired, and from the sound of it, you could use a good night's sleep too. Why don't we call it a night and reconnect this weekend?"

Now that I had him back and sitting in the same booth as me, I didn't want to let him out of my sight.

How else can I protect him? It is up to me.

"Are you sure, Will? You don't want to get another beer before we go?"

"You know me, RJ. I'm not gonna risk the drive home. Besides, I'm looking at apartments tomorrow morning, so I should probably get outta here."

I gave in and paid for our beers, and we walked out together.

"Which way are you parked?" I asked.

"Over by the parking lot they use for the farmer's market," he replied, pointing.

"Okay, I'm somewhat over that way, by the stand-up comedy place, so I'll walk with you for a bit."

It was a warm June night and relatively quiet on the city streets; after all, it was a Monday. Aside from the general din of normal traffic, we walked to the soundtrack of Will's brown flip-flops' rhythmic slapping against the bottoms of his feet.

When we reached the point where I was to veer right toward the surface lot where my car sat, we did the typical handshake/hug, except this time, *he* held on for an extra beat and said, "Hey, man,

I know you said you're worried about me, but I'm fine. I'm better than fine. I am in such a good place right now, but I'm more worried about *you*. Something seems really off right now, so I just want *you* to take care of *yourself*, alright?"

I simply nodded.

He concluded, "You are a great friend, and I love you, bro."

Neither of us had ever used that word. It just wasn't something you said, you know? Perhaps it was *known*, but it was never said. Perhaps he knew I needed to hear it.

"I appreciate that. Love you too, buddy."

With that, he nodded and broke the moment with, "Cool, cool. I'll call you later in the week, and we can figure out getting together this weekend. I'd love to see Ann too."

"That'd be great. Drive carefully."

"Yep, you too." And we parted ways.

As the smacking of his flip-flops grew increasingly distant, I watched him walk, grateful for having had the talk we had. Grateful to have him back again. Grateful for the peace I felt in him. Grateful for the peace of the quiet night.

All peace was shattered in an instant. As Will crossed Third Avenue toward the farmer's market parking lot, a rusty Ford Econoline van sped straight through the adjacent four-way stop intersection; the driver never even tapped the break prior to colliding squarely with the entirety of my best friend's body, sending him hurling limply through the air and landing with an unspeakable sound on the cement curb.

I screamed and ran the block and a half toward the spot. The van driver slammed his breaks *after* the impact and, leaving his van in the middle of the street, staggered out with his hands on his backward green baseball hat, tears welling in his red eyes and whiskey emanating from his goateed mouth.

Dad, I can't get into describing what it looked like—what *he* looked like lying on the curb. I'm too tired of describing these scenes to you. Most people go their whole lives never having to see anything so horrible; I was seeing it repeatedly. My best friend was mowed down fifty yards away from me while I watched helplessly. These are images that haunt people for the rest of their lives, and I am no exception. I've run out of ways to write the word *pain*.

I yelled at the drunk to call 911. He hesitated, apparently having enough clarity in the moment to realize that he would be calling the same folks who would lock him up. "Call 911!" I repeated. He stood and stared, slowly shaking his head. I was about to pull out my cell phone when I saw a short, thin black woman in her forties running toward us with her phone up to her ear already. I tried to hold Will, but there wasn't a clear way *to* hold him. I also remembered what they always say about not moving someone who may have a broken neck, so I hovered above and around him and told him that help was on the way. I couldn't touch him. I couldn't move him. I couldn't make the bleeding stop, fix the angles of body parts, or rebuild the side of his head. I was utterly helpless. I sat next to him, trying not to lose consciousness, and I wept.

It wasn't until help arrived that I emerged from my emotional cloud to realize that the Econoline driver had quietly poured himself back into his van and left prior to law enforcement's arrival. I later gathered that the woman who had called for help also got the license plate information for the police. A swarm of flashing lights and wailing sirens arrived seemingly in unison, closed off the area, and got to work on Will. At one point, minutes into the scene, the bodies in uniforms transitioned from frenetic to calm. Resigned. Police spoke into the receivers on their shoulders as they prepared the area for the investigation of what was now a crime scene. Cloths were brought out to cover Will's body.

Officers asked me questions, and I did my best to help. My head spun. They asked if I had a way of contacting Will's family. I threw up on the sidewalk.

I reluctantly pulled up Mrs. H's number from my contacts and pressed my Nokia with a shaking thumb. She answered quickly, and I wept into the phone.

"I couldn't save him! I tried!" I yelled, sniffling hard to stop snot from streaming into my mouth. "Will was hit by a van tonight. They couldn't save him. I couldn't save him. I am so sorry."

SAVING WILL

I would give *anything* to erase that moment—having to hear a mother's screaming collapse after hearing from her youngest son's friend that he was mowed down. The life she started was erased twenty-six years later, and on the other end of her phone, I was the one holding the eraser. Likewise, I'd give anything not to hear the fear in Mr. Hogan's voice in the background as she tried to relay the news to him while he held her in his arms on the kitchen floor. That moment. I wanted it to go away.

At some point, I handed my phone to the officer, who talked with Mr. Hogan for several minutes. About what? I didn't recall; I wasn't really *there* at that point. After we watched uniformed men hoist Will's covered body into the back of an ambulance, the officer who had used my phone to speak to Mr. Hogan turned to me.

"Are you okay to drive home?"

"Yes, sir. I'm not drunk or anything."

"I didn't think you *were*," he responded. "I meant *emotionally* okay to drive home. You wanna call someone and get a lift?" he said, gesturing with his eyes to my wedding ring.

"Oh, right."

Ann. I have to tell her again.

I hesitated, then continued, "No. I'll be okay. I'd rather just get home to tell her in person."

"Okay, buddy," the officer said, pursing his lips. "We have all your contact information. You're likely to hear from our department as the investigation into the driver moves along. We'll do everything we can to find this guy."

I nodded.

He concluded, "I'm very sorry about your friend."

I nodded again and turned to walk the block and a half to my car.

If only Will had parked in the same lot...

If I had convinced him to stay for another drink...

If I had picked him up on my way here...

Three thoughts and thirty yards into my walk, I stopped. I crouched down to get a better look at a brown object on the concrete that caught my eye, and then slowly lifted Will's sandal. I held it with both hands, thinking about how his right foot had just been in it mere moments prior and thinking about how far it flew from where he was run down.

Do I save it?
Would Mr. and Mrs. Hogan want it?
Where's the other *one?*

I looked from side to side but couldn't find its counterpart. It might have still been on his foot; this wasn't a detail I cataloged that night. Not knowing what else to do with it, I carried it back to my Grand Prix, gently placed it on the floor on the passenger side and continued to stare at it for several ticks before putting the keys in the ignition to begin my short journey back to the condo. Ann would be waiting, and I'd have to break her heart all over again as mine lay on the mat, like a boxer not wanting to get back up once more.

The conversation was crushing, of course, and littered with confusion. Anytime I caught my breath from crying, I repeated the refrain, "I tried to save him, but I couldn't," which led to her probing what that meant.

"Did you do CPR or something?" she asked, and I muttered confusing answers.

"Honey," she cautiously started, "those things you said yesterday about Will dying…how did you *know* he was going to die?"

I was afraid to tell my truth again. I knew it would lead to the "you need to get help" conversation again. It was a crossroads, where I could choose to double down on the seemingly delusional account I'd told the day before and drag my bride into this dark hell I'd been swirling in, or I could preemptively release her from it and bear the burden—for however long it would last—alone. It was exhausting to consider trying to bring her along with my truth (*what could she* do *about it anyway?*) and I felt it might somehow make my grief worse, not better. So I swallowed it all. A day after unloading everything on her, in that moment, I decided to take it all back.

"That was all just a dream I had," was all I could think to respond.

"That's not how you talked about it yesterday after Will called you."

"I was just going through some stuff, Ann. Just forget it. It was just a dream. I'm done talking like that. I'm done talking about that. Right now, I just need you to support me through this…" I concluded, barely avoiding saying the word "again" to end that sentence.

She complied. We stopped talking about how I couldn't save him. We sat and cried together until we were dry. I'm sure she thought about it thereafter, but she never again brought it up. Neither did I.

*****

The next morning, I jolted awake, not out of fear or because of a nightmare (this time), but because I was awake and felt a surge of energy for the day. It didn't make any sense, really. I should have moped, not showered, called in sick to work, and made dozens of painful phone calls to Will's friends. Instead, I skipped out of bed, brushed my teeth, and decided to go for a dawn run through our condo subdivision. As a former athlete, I decided to try to "walk it off." Or, in this case, run it off.

The June morning air was perfectly crisp for running, and it didn't take long for me to transition from a casual warm-up pace to an angry best-friend-just-died (again) therapeutic pace. I exited our sub and headed south, adjacent to the main road, traveling at a truly unsustainable pace. I glided across the next half mile of uneven sidewalk without a thought. I just ran and wiped tears from my eyes and cheeks. My tunnel vision was broken when the blur of a chipmunk darted from a set of shrubs and into the path of my right foot's next stride. I quickly diverted my step to avoid crushing the fuzzy brown creature, only to have my foot land on the right edge of the crooked sidewalk, sending my ankle sideways. It rolled hard.

As you know, Dad, I had rolled and sprained my ankles so many times playing soccer that I lost count and had to have the Mitchell College athletic training staff tape my ankles before every practice and game for my last two years of college ball. This history did not make my ankle hurt any less as I rolled onto the grassy easement; it *did* give me enough knowledge to recognize that it wasn't broken. It was the same damn feeling I'd had many times before, but that didn't make it any easier to slowly retrace my steps back home. I felt every careful step on my right foot. Where my long, effortless, quick strides to get to the intersection of me and the chipmunk were mostly free of deep thought, the short, belabored, slow hobbles back toward our condo were weighed down with heavy contemplation and a sudden and shattering realization.

He died at the scene.
He died instantly.
No life support.
No hushed meeting or paperwork signing by the Hogans at a hospital.
No organ donations.

I ceased my limp and fell into a seated position, with the noodle legs of a toddler refusing to be picked up, on the curb facing the convenience store just outside the entrance to our condo complex. With my forehead pressed against the interlocked palms of both hands, I broke down as I thought of Gabi—her college dream, her band, her loving family, and her sudden fear of snakes. And Malcolm, watching beautiful Kameron play the violin—tears flowing from his newly-working eyes. And Dr. Anderson. Ugh, Dr. Anderson—his beautiful family, his heart dedicated to operating on those children—all in question. And Keith—not the best character around, but one who seemed to have tried and whose health and life could be turned around. And the fifth one, nameless, unknown.

Did we lose them all *last night?*

As I sat like a pile of dirty laundry, my throbbing ankle forced me to think of the chipmunk. If he hadn't darted out right at that moment, if I hadn't left the house exactly when I did, if I hadn't seen him and merely stepped on him and crushed him, or if I had unknowingly strode right over him, I wouldn't have been in so much pain. If I wasn't in pain, I wouldn't have limped home and perhaps wouldn't have had time to think about any of this.

My answered prayers to get Will back once more, to have another chance to save him, resulted in unanswered prayers for many others.

Who am I to decide who lives and dies?

Who am I to decide if a person is worthy of a second chance at life, whether their "story" is good enough, and whether they are a good enough person to deserve it?

Do any of us deserve anything we have?

Another year to live, another week with our kids, another sunset, another alarm clock, another breath?

I collected myself and limped the rest of the way back to the condo, where I iced my ankle and called in sick for work.

*****

Of course, there was the funeral. Again. This time, it was a closed casket—no baseball hat would do what would have been required. The rest was mostly a replay. ("He's in a better place.") For the first time, I didn't hear, "As tough as this is, I'm glad his organs were able to go to five different people. Such a blessing for them." His brother-in-law delivered the same beautiful words. I froze in my seat when the time came to speak, lamenting that I'd have to write it all down for Mrs. Hogan yet again. Carrying the casket. The miles-long line of vehicles snaking through the winding cemetery roads. And profound, profound sadness.

*****

The months that followed were not a replay, and my sadness would grow to newfound, deeper levels. He wasn't coming back. I waited, ready. But he wasn't coming back as he had before. As my hopes to see him again and have one more chance faded as the summer green leaves faded to yellow, my thoughts turned to the others I'd met. I had to know what became of them. Surely other donors were out there, I kept reminding myself.

Thanks to the same photographic memory that served me well in studying for college exams, I remembered Malcolm's and Keith's respective addresses. Coupled with remembering Sam's Family Diner in St. Louis and knowing I could find Dr. Anderson in his hospital's directory, I had a way of getting to all four I'd previously met.

I told Ann I was going back to Mitchel College for the annual alumni soccer game. Instead, I drove past the exit to Mitchel and got off two exits later to head to St. Louis, Michigan. It was crazy to think how close Gabi was to where I spent my formative years and where I met Will.

Remembering Gabi's sister Alma's nametag and simply hoping for the best, I pulled into Sam's Family Diner to connect to her, the only way I could think of without having her call the cops on a psychotic stalker. The restaurant's chipped red paint, wood siding, and thirty-year-old sign greeted me as I reached for the door handle. This was the kind of town and restaurant where, when a stranger walks through the front door, everyone in the place knows it. I felt every face in there asking, "You're not from around here, are you?" It was too late for lunch and too early for dinner, so Sam's was quiet enough to hear silverware clinking plates from the few patrons who enjoyed their meals. My heart raced when Alma stepped out of the kitchen, carrying a huge tray of food for a family of five in the far corner booth. She appeared to be the only server working, so I didn't have to worry about where to sit. The hostess interrupted my gaze.

"For one?"

"What? Oh, yeah. Sorry. Just me, yeah."

"Booth or table?"

"Either way."

"Okay, right this way," she said as she grabbed one menu from the stack. "Your first time here," she said in a way resembling more of a statement than a question.

"Yes. What's good?"

"Oh, everything. But our burgers are our specialty," she added as she sat me in a booth not far from the front entrance, wished me a good first meal at Sam's, and finished with, "Alma will be your server and will be right with you."

Alma Dominguez headed my way after unloading the last of the heavy tray for the booth family across the way, her jet-black hair pulled tightly back in a bun. It's the strangest thing to see someone you've met and with whom you've shared tears and hugs walking your way with a facial expression of one hundred percent nondescript daily work routine. She forced a smile as she approached my booth.

"I'm Alma. I'll be taking care of you today. Can I get you started with anything other than water?"

"No, I'm good with just water."

Every ounce of me wanted to ask how she, her parents, and, most importantly, Gabi were doing. But again, I had to avoid having her call the cops because of some crazy out-of-towner overdue for a shave, claiming to know her and her whole family—especially in that small of a town where the cops probably actually *did* know her and her whole family. It was then that I realized I had no plan. You'd think the two-hour drive would have given me time to cook something up but making that drive up right by Mitchel College just had me reliving a lot of those memories, and I hadn't even thought of what to say once I got there. So, it was just show-up-and-hope-for-the-best.

"Do you want another minute to look over the menu?"

"That would be good."

"Okay, no rush. I'll come back and check on you in a couple minutes."

I watched her as she checked in on the other four tables of diners at Sam's. It turned out the smile she forced for me wasn't unique to me as an out-of-towner. Her smiles also seemed painfully forced for all the locals she clearly knew. As promised, she circled back to me after refilling water at one table, replacing dropped silverware at another, and bringing the bill for a silver-haired couple at a third.

"You all set to order?"

"Yeah, I'll have the all-American burger with the seasoned fries."

"Alright, I'll get that right up for you," she said, while making no eye contact and collecting the menu back from me.

"Thanks, Alma."

After minutes of people-watching, reading some local newsletter, and overall losing track of time and surroundings, a young woman with badly dyed straight blonde hair I'd never seen delivered my burger and fries. I must have given her a puzzled look.

"I'm Mandy. I'm taking over for Alma this afternoon. How does everything look?" she added, looking down at the meal she'd just delivered.

"Oh, um," I looked down. "It looks good. So, Alma left?"

"Yeah, she had a, uh, thing to go to today, but I'll take good care of you."

"Is she okay?"

She paused, eyeing me over, no doubt suspicious of my line of questioning and wondering when I'd shut up and eat my all-American burger and seasoned fries. At that point, the "You're not from around here, are you?" look on her face converted to actual words spoken aloud.

"You're not from St. Louis, then, huh?"

"That's right. Just passing through today. I'm sorry if I—"

"Do you know Alma?"

"Yeah, somewhat—it's...it's complicated actually."

"Alma's sister is really sick," she interjected abruptly. "The church is hosting a special prayer service for her today at three, so that's why she had to leave."

I paused. Nodded. "I'm really sorry to hear that. Really sorry."

She got quieter. "So is there anything else I can get for you right now other than the burger and fries?"

"No, I'm good. Thank you, though."

I grabbed the burger and took my first bite, stared into the middle distance, and wondered if I could even eat it given the pit now residing in my stomach. Halfway through my plate—the burger *was* good, by the way, despite my sudden lack of appetite—I checked my watch and resolved to find the church and attend the service thirty minutes later.

The good news was in a small town like that, there was a reason someone would say that *"the"* church was hosting a prayer vigil. I quickly found the church on the main road—a rounded red brick Presbyterian church with a white steeple and vines crawling up the east wall—based on it being the first church I saw and the cars packing the side parking lot and lining the main street. A church this busy on a random Saturday afternoon had to be the one I was looking for. I pulled into the half-full parking lot of the single-screen movie theater across the street, walked under the rather dingy marquee promoting *The Day After Tomorrow* and *The Butterfly Effect*—complete with the frozen Statue of Liberty arm and Ashton Kutcher posters, respectively—and apprehensively crossed the street to the church.

The worries I had about being questioned as an outsider disappeared when I walked through the white double doors. The place was packed, and folks were scrambling to exchange hugs and find their seats as the program was set to begin. A light-brown-skinned and black-robed man walked away from a group of huggers until he was behind the lectern at the front of the twenty rows of jammed pews.

In a lightly Mexican-accented English, he called the crowd of multiple skin tones to order with a simple, "Please be seated." The hushed speaking tones faded into silence as everyone found a spot. "Thank you all for coming. We all know why we are gathered here today. We are gathered because one of our own needs help, and we know the power of prayer. *Dios provee.* As you all know, Gabriella Dominguez is very ill. She couldn't be here today, but her *madre y padre* are here, as well as her sister, Alma. They will say a few words in a moment."

The pastor paused, looked at Gabi's family, glanced down at the lectern, shuffled some papers, and then quietly continued into the microphone.

"Let us pray. *Dejanos rezar.*" Deep, resolute breath. "Heavenly Father, we give thanks for this glorious, sunny day you have made. We give thanks for safe travels for everyone here today and for each of them being here today. God, you are a God of *provision* and a God of the *miraculous.* Our sister in Christ, Gabriella Dominguez, needs a miracle. You've numbered every hair on our respective heads, and you know our prayers before we even pray them. You know she needs a new kidney very soon, and through what some today call the miracle of modern medicine, we know you have equipped mankind with the ability to save her. If it is her time to be with you, Lord…

we accept this. We want more time with Gabi on this earth. She is a bright, vibrant, and beautiful soul, Lord. She has much left to do. To give. To live. We pray for peace for the Dominguez family during this difficult time. But most of all, we pray to you, God, to save Gabi. In the same way you gave your people eight days' worth of fire when their lamp oil only allowed for one, we pray for your miraculous hand. In the same way you fed five thousand through your son, Jesus Christ, with only two fish and five loaves of bread, we pray for your miraculous hand to touch your child, Gabi. In the same way you rose Lazarus from the dead, we pray you will cause Gabi's name to rise to the top of the list of donor kidney matches. If a donation is not your will, we pray your healing hand will miraculously heal Gabi and make her one hundred percent well again…We pray this in the redeeming, loving, *healing* name of your son, Jesus Christ, our Lord. Amen."

Amens echoed from the congregation.

The pastor—who never introduced himself because, presumably, everyone already knew him—gathered his loose papers from the lectern and nodded toward Gabi's family. Still wearing her black work uniform, Alma stood up nervously and made her way out of the front pew to take her place in front of the gathering.

After a deep breath in and out, she began, "Thank you all for being here. Gabi sends her love and appreciation too." Her voice cracked on her sister's name. "I speak today on behalf of her and on behalf of my parents. You all know how special my sister is. That's why you're here. And my family and I thank you for your prayers today and for all your prayers in all these past weeks and months. The right kidney for Gabi is out there. I know it…"

She trailed off and looked lost as to what to say next, glancing side to side, seemingly hoping someone would bail her out. Someone must have signaled her because she snapped back to the program. "Oh, yeah. I guess now we are going to hand out candles to light."

Several twenty-somethings flanked the pews with baskets of thin white candles wrapped halfway down in clear discs. They handed out the candles in an orderly way, then circled back to light the aisle seat candles in each row, starting a chain of attendees paying that forward—or left and right, as it were—to include my candle being lit in my position in the far back right pew.

The pastor stood again in front of the group. "As was written by the prophet Isaiah, 'Do not fear, for I am with you; do not be dismayed, for I am your God. I will strengthen you and help you; I will uphold you with my righteous right hand.'" With these last words, he raised the candle in his right hand. "Now I ask you all to join me in a silent prayer for the healing of our sister in Christ, Gabriella."

Silence.

Heads bowed.

Eyes closed.

Silence.

I didn't know what to pray *for*. I was the only person under that roof—or anywhere else, for that matter—who knew that the miracle kidney they all prayed for was destroyed by a drunk on a Monday night months before. If that was the option we prayed for, what was the sense in joining that prayer?

Instead, I slumped and looked down at my burning candle.

Silence.

Hot wax began to pool at the top until it could no longer pool. Drops traveled down the white stem until resting on the clear plastic disc, which sat on the webbing between my right thumb and index finger.

So strange to see hot wax on top of my flesh but not be able to feel a thing.

Longest silent prayer ever.

I tilted the candle to encourage more wax to run onto the disc on my right hand. The wax complied. Soon, the pool of hot wax resting on the plastic resting on my hand was the size of a half-dollar. I thought of sitting with Will in his dorm room with lit matches, seeing if we could say the Greek alphabet from alpha to omega twice before the flame reached our fingers. The skin on our thumbs and index fingers suffered a poor fate on more than one occasion before we grew to Aristotle-like proficiency.

Eyes positively glazed over, I thought of purposely burning myself with the hot wax—again, just to ensure all was *real*—to know I was alive.

"Amen."

I shook my head quickly from side to side as the word snapped me back to the red brick church in mid-Michigan. There was more to the service, I'm sure, but those are the parts I remember best. Oh, and my hasty exit. The Dominguez family was excused first so they could greet folks on the way out the door—wedding-style. I tried to flow out of there unnoticed with a group of twenty-somethings, but as I walked behind the group to slide out, Alma caught my eye. She had the look of, well, someone who waited on a stranger at a restaurant, left her shift early to attend a prayer vigil for her dying sister, and then saw the said stranger *attend* the said prayer vigil. There was nothing to say. While her eyes creased and her head tilted to the right like a Labrador puppy, I nodded her way to acknowledge the shared eye contact and picked up my pace across Main Street toward the theater.

From my Grand Prix, I placed my hands on top of the steering wheel and watched the family I knew (who didn't know me) hug, handshake, and cry with the dozens of small-town folks making their way out of the building. I turned my hands off the wheel and looked at the disorganized lines in the skin of my right palm for a moment, then back up at the family in time to see the church doors shut behind them as they walked back in.

I turned the key in the ignition and drove the two hours home.

*****

Weeks later, nothing had changed. Will wasn't coming back. Things got darker for me. More episodes, like the one with the razor and the hot wax, followed. I didn't know how to get out of it. Despite wanting to hurt myself, I didn't think I would have taken my own life. I had too much to do, and I would never do that to Ann. Plus, I had to be there in case I had another chance to save Will. It was dark, which I think was why I continued to pursue seeing the others. It hurt me, but that's what I was into at that point.

It also hurt me to lie to Ann, but that's what I did more and more in those days.

"I'm fine."

"I'm not hungry because I had a big late lunch."

"I have a training meeting in New York next week."

I pulled out this last big lie to set up my road trip to see Malcolm Reems in Indiana and Keith Young in Ohio. I didn't think I could pull off yet another weekend away from Ann without serious marital consequences, so the likely story of a midweek training session worked well. I left on a Tuesday morning with no plan other than to plug the addresses that I absurdly remembered into a mapping website and just show up.

I headed to Indy first to see Hank Aaron's old teammate. I braced myself for the entire four-and-a-half-hour drive.

What will I see?

What will he see?

After only one bathroom break, I pulled into Malcolm Reems' familiar, cozy neighborhood.

I cannot believe I drove four-plus hours just to stalk this guy from my car.

What do I expect to see?

I can't imagine I'll talk to him.

I crept past his house. All was quiet.

Now what?

I parked next to the curb several houses down from his, sighed, and pulled out the book I had packed for entertainment later that night in whatever hotel room I would find. After an hour, I left to get some drive-thru food to bring back to my stakeout spot. About forty minutes after licking the last of the french-fry salt off my fingers, Ronald and LaSonja's familiar Ford Explorer pulled into Malcolm's driveway. My heart raced.

Ronald stepped out of the vehicle, walked around, and opened the passenger door. Tan-panted legs swung out, and black New

Balance sneakers connected to the cracked concrete. Ronald took the elder Reems by the left elbow and guided him out of the SUV. Malcolm wore sunglasses and carried a thin cane. Ronald's hold on his father's elbow continued until he guided him up onto the front porch and into the seat of a glider. After a brief exchange of words, Ronald disappeared into the home. Alone, Malcolm looked straight ahead, still. Minutes later, Ronald emerged through the light blue front door with two glasses of lemonade.

Must be their family's drink of choice.

They sat together and talked, but mostly just sat. After they both seemed content with where their discussion landed or with where the silence sat, Ronald put his hands on his knees, leaned forward in his seat, and rose to leave. He seemed to offer his dad help into the house, but Malcolm waved him off. Both men said goodbye, and Ronald drove the Explorer out of sight. The former big-leaguer faced the street and massaged the top of his cane with his palms.

I got out of my car. I had to stretch my legs before driving as far as I could toward Norwalk anyway, so I figured I'd walk through Malcolm's neighborhood. As I walked, I watched him the whole way, wondering if he would look my way and what I would say if he greeted me. I paused in front of his house, my heart beating a little harder. He continued to face straight ahead. Without knowing what I would say if engaged in dialogue, I waved.

Nothing.

I told myself his eyes were closed behind those sunglasses for a quick old-man-sitting-on-a-porch nap. But as I stood watching him, he continued to rub the top of his cane. He then swatted a mosquito off his forearm. He was very much awake.

And very much *blind*.

I continued to stand no more than twenty-five yards from his stoop, my hands now in my pockets, observing Malcolm, trying to piece time back together from its splintered existence in my head. This was now many months after what would have been the time I had met him, Ronald, LaSonja, and beautiful Kameron (and her violin).

I can't believe how quickly this progressed.

Wait, what am I thinking? I never saw what he was like before *the transplant.*

Unable to stand there much longer, I quietly turned and continued down the sidewalk farther away from my car—my head down and eyes on the concrete, which was losing its battle against a superhighway of grass-filled cracks. One house away. Then two houses away. Then, whistling. I heard the faint, but familiar, whistling from my eight o'clock. I stopped, turned around, and looked for the source.

Of course, it was coming from the porch in front of the light blue front door; otherwise, I likely wouldn't have included the detail in this letter. Still massaging the butt of the cane, Malcolm now raised his head slightly beyond horizontal, his wrinkled cheeks drawn in slightly, his lips pursed. It was the familiar tune his granddaughter played on her violin while Alex and I sipped lemonade in his backyard, listening to the rest of his family sing the words, "Amazing grace, how sweet the sound that saved a wretch like me. I once was lost but now I'm found. Was blind, but now I see."

Tears gathered in the corners of my eyes. Malcolm concluded one verse of the melody, nodded as a man does when he's completed a task from his to-do list, turned, and found his way through the light blue door into his home that shut behind him with a bang. In turn, I pivoted to continue my leg-stretching walk through the neighborhood, buried deep in thought throughout.

What must the words to that melody mean to him now?

"Was blind, but now I see"?

How can he still whistle that tune?

He once could see, but now he's blind.

He once could see well enough to play professional baseball, *but now he's blind.*

I completed the loop around the block and settled back into my Pontiac's driver's seat. The porch Malcolm left remained empty. The glider still nodded ever so slightly toward the street and back. I placed the MapQuest printout that would guide me from suburban Indianapolis to Norwalk, Ohio, on the passenger seat and put the car in drive. As I rolled slowly past his house, I caught one last glimpse of the glass patio table in the backyard where Alex and I once sipped lemonade.

*****

I pulled into a cheap hotel near Norwalk around midnight and used cash to pay for the room, so Ann wouldn't later see it on our credit card statement. I didn't feel great about lying to Ann. But there was a lot I didn't feel great about. To include drinking the Captain and Coke I brought from home alone in my hotel room that night until I couldn't exactly see straight. Will was a whiskey man; I could never stand the smell or taste, but rum became, at times, my best friend and worst enemy. That night, somewhere outside Norwalk, it was the friend I needed to help me forget. And in the morning, it was an enemy reminding me I never would.

After showering off the stink and shame from the prior night and swallowing a fistful of anti-inflammatories, I followed the previous day's blueprint: use MapQuest printouts to get back to unit 17E of Keith Young's Walnut Creek apartment complex and see what would happen next. I pulled into the nondescript entry and wound to the back of the property.

As with the previous day's attempt, there was no immediate payoff. Keith's rusty blue Ford Ranger was in the same 17E-reserved spot it was the previous time we met, but I wasn't going to buzz up to his apartment—especially not this guy, after seeing how "rough around the edges" he was when Alex and I met him. He wasn't exactly soft and cuddly when he knew he was meeting the brother and friend of the young man whose liver resided in his body. I couldn't imagine his response if a stranger randomly buzzed his apartment to hear about how his life was going, sans the liver. So, I waited. A lot.

After many boring minutes found me alternating between reading my book and people-watching around the apartment complex, I noticed there was something different about his truck. It took me a minute to figure it out. It was a piece of junk, just like it was the previous time.

What is it?

I pulled my Grand Prix forward into the parking spot closer to the buildings to get a better look from a different angle.

The front fender was heavily dented, and the right front headlight was shattered.

That's new.

No one came out of 17E for hours. I ran up to Wendy's for lunch. Went back. Read the first eighty-or-so pages of the book, *A Million Little Pieces*. Responded to emails on my laptop.

Wait, why is his truck even here? It's midmorning on a weekday.

This was a weekday. He had a job. I thought of that dirty white "All-Star Plumbing, Heating, and Cooling" T-shirt. More sitting, listening to the radio, and observing random apartment dwellers coming and going. A young mother was pushing a stroller. An apartment employee was dragging a toolbox in and out of one of the buildings repeatedly. Two older women were walking side-by-side, both staring at the sidewalk.

Just as dinner hunger pangs began—as did my doubt that I'd see Keith—a late-model Nissan Something-or-Other rumbled to a stop in front of Keith's building. Thinning blonde hair and a dirty white T-shirt emerged from the passenger door. He gave a nod to the unseen driver, who pulled away. Keith walked to the bench where Alex and I once sat with him. He sat, lit a cigarette between his fingers, and rested his elbows on his thighs. He took a long, puckered drag from his cancer stick and slowly let out the cloud. Rinse and repeat. Halfway through his work on the flame between his knees, he paused his routine, slid his right hand into a brown paper bag I hadn't noticed until then, and pulled from it a pint of Captain Morgan. New routine: drag, blow, swig. He must have finished half the pint by the time he finished the second half of the smoke.

I guess he's back to drinking. Maybe he never left it.

He gave himself time for a few clean breaths after the routine before pulling his Nokia out of the paper bag and dialing. He leaned back and appeared to take a big "here we go" breath before hitting SEND. I cracked my window and strained to listen, but I was far enough away to hear only tone, not words. Keith did most of the talking with whomever was on the other end. His tone was strained. Then remorseful. Then pleading. And finally, resigned.

END.

A broken man set the Nokia on top of the paper bag.

He bit his lower lip, tilted his head back against the metal bench, and then uncapped the bottle for another longer pull. He then abruptly grabbed the phone and bottle and headed toward his building, letting himself in with his key and disappearing into the hall of his building when the teal door shut behind him. He left the brown paper bag on the bench for someone else to deal with later.

That was it. That was all I saw of Keith. I didn't know for sure who he spoke with on the phone that day, but you and I both know it was his daughter. And it didn't go well.

*****

The dull darkness of each day hung around my neck. I was in quicksand. I couldn't stop thinking about Will. I couldn't stop thinking about the others. I couldn't stop questioning myself. I couldn't stop questioning God.

The others.

Of course, there were the four.

But there was also the fifth.

The selfish person who couldn't be bothered to meet, and perhaps even *thank*, the family of the one whose sacrifice led to his or her new pancreas and second chance at life. That person was part of all I thought about in those weeks. One cloudy morning, I sat in a coffee shop, waiting for a work colleague to meet me, and looked past my laptop to the dozen-ish people sipping lattes and eating carbs and sugar.

A man and woman, each with graying hair, were holding both of each other's hands across the table where their lattes steamed.

SAVING WILL

A mother and her two teenage sons were silently sipping something.

Two attractive women in business suits huddled around printed reports.

A round-faced octogenarian donned a WWII veteran's cap, spread a newspaper wide over his folded leg. He quickly folding the paper to the side when a similarly-appearing man pulled up with his black coffee to join him in discussing the day's current events.

I was not sure why it was that day in that coffee shop, but knowledge grew up in me as if scales had been removed from my eyes.

Everyone I see has a pancreas.

Every one of them.

Any one of them could have someone else's pancreas in them.

And any one of them could have Will's *pancreas inside them.*

If one of the WWII vets griping about the Tigers' starting pitching rotation had Will's pancreas working inside him to crank out beta cells to allow his body to metabolize sugar and allow him to continue to gripe, grieve, or rejoice, would I think of him differently? Would I maybe go over to talk to him? Would I have let him cut in line to get his coffee?

Are the woman and her teenage sons so quiet because of teenage angst, or is it something more? Are they waiting for a test result to come back? Are they mourning the loss of their father? Are they silently and humbly thankful that she has beaten the odds, thanks to her new pancreas? And, if so, then what? Would I buy them breakfast? Would I ask her if she's now inexplicably afraid of snakes?

A group of three forty-something women found a small round table with two chairs. They looked around for another option. I jumped to my feet, grabbed the other chair at my table, and walked it over there.

"Here. You can use this one if you need it."

"Oh, thank you so much," the brunette replied. "That was so nice."

It wasn't until I returned to my laptop that I recognized that my work colleague would now have nowhere to sit when she arrived.

So that was the day I saw coffee shops differently. And restaurants. And stores. And traffic jams. Everyone around me had Will's pancreas. Or, at least, they theoretically *could* have had Will's pancreas. And that was how I started acting. It might have been a desperate attempt, among the *many* desperate attempts I'd been making for months, to keep him with me—*around* me—every day. You could call it an optimistic delusion, I suppose. Whatever it might have been, I could say with certainty what it was for me: a gift.

At a time when I sought comfort in the numbing balm found at the bottom of a bottle, this pointed my attention externally. Everyone around me suddenly had a bit of Will's spirit with them, and that kept him around. At least a little bit. And it probably made me a little easier to be around. I just wish it made me happier to be around myself.

*****

The subsequent days included work, little sleep, and me lying to Ann about how my supposed business trip had gone.

After Will's death, I picked up the dim hobby of reading obituaries; all of them interested me, but I was particularly drawn to younger people. It always upsets me when the cause of death isn't part of the article.

Young people don't just die; *you have to tell us* why.

I liked reading about WWII vets and the honorable lives they lived, even *after* their great service to our country. With every obituary of an older person, though, I dwelled on why they got those eighty- or ninety-plus years and Will didn't. No level of literary license could cover up the fact that some of these people were simply unremarkable, and I was positive that Will's next sixty-plus years would have been anything but unremarkable. Months after Will's death, there was one obituary that sent me to the deepest depths of that dark hole.

> *A skilled surgeon who is remembered most as a loving son, husband, and father. Trevor Anderson, age forty, of Bloomfield Hills, Michigan, died on Sunday evening, surrounded by family. He is survived by*

his wife, Kelly; children, Emma (eight) and Owen (five); grandmother, Ruth; parents, Ted and Denise; brother Randy (Samantha); and nieces, Opal (four) and Isabella (two). Born and raised in metro Detroit, he proudly never left, having completed undergraduate studies at the University of Michigan, medical school at Wayne State University, a surgery residency at the Detroit Medical Center, and a pediatric surgery fellowship back at the University of Michigan. Trevor met the love of his life, Kelly, at a football game in Ann Arbor, and the two were married in 1988. He was a devoted father to Emma and Owen and a passionate surgeon for every child he ever served. Services will be held this Saturday at 2:00 p.m. at the Hinkley Brothers Funeral Home in Birmingham. Memorial donations can be made to the St. Stephen's Hospital Pediatric Surgery Center or the Heart Failure Society of America.

He didn't make it. There must not have been any other appropriate donor matches in time to save him. My chest ached for Kelly, Emma, and Owen. It hurt, too, that I really couldn't talk to anyone about this loss. No one else would understand the connection that only I knew. Even Alex wouldn't have known he met them because, in his reality, he *didn't* meet them. After much deliberation over the rest of the week, I decided to make up an excuse to be gone at 2:00 on Saturday—to pay my respects to someone who never knew he met me and never knew the chance he might have had at a second chance.

*****

Having discretely thrown a suit in the trunk of my car and telling Ann I had to help my parents move some things out of their garage, I dressed the part in a McDonald's parking lot and awkwardly approached the Hinkley Brothers Funeral Home just before 2:00—nearly late after having to park several blocks away. The service was late to start anyway, as countless forlorn faces patiently crammed into the large room where Dr. Anderson lay. One couldn't help noticing numerous kids and young adults interspersed with well-dressed medical professionals, sitting on black folding chairs, and standing around the edges of the room among flowers and photo boards—with me amid the latter.

Kelly, Emma, and Owen sat in the front row with what looked to be his parents, grandmother, and his younger brother and his family. Owen held a superhero action figure as the service began with words from a white-haired and bearded minister in a black robe. He was a bit heavy-set. He regularly paused to allow silence to speak for him, and he emphasized important words by holding up his meaty right hand with his palm raised and moving his fingers in a way that looked like he was trying to clean an invisible crystal ball. His made-for-radio voice boomed even when he wasn't projecting, and he pronounced "God" as "Gawd," even though nothing else he said seemed to indicate an accent congruent with that pronunciation. He was never introduced; he merely walked to the lectern next to Dr. Anderson's casket and began.

"On behalf of Kelly and the entire Anderson family, thank you all for being here today," he started. "Looking around this large room, it is clear to anyone just how beloved Dr. Trevor Anderson was. And I know he loved all of you right back." These opening words drew coughs and sniffles from the sea of black dress clothes.

"Days like today represent one of the hardest things I do in my work, particularly when the one we've lost presumably had so much left to give the world…but it is also my honor to be here to glorify God in all we do and say this afternoon." He paused for a sip of water, then intentionally scanned the room from his left to his right. "I look out at all your beautiful faces—created by God himself in his own image—and I see pain. I see sadness. And, frankly, I see skepticism as well. Doubt. Anger. My guess is that some of you—maybe *many* of you—fall into the ever-growing category of 'not religious.'"

Yes, he used his fingers to make "air quotes."

"And now you've come to mourn the loss of your way-too-young friend, coworker, family member, heroic surgeon…and there's an old man in a robe talking about glorifying God. 'Why would any god allow such a good man—one who was such a blessing to so many others—to be taken from us so soon?' is what I'm sure you may be thinking... You aren't the first people to think this...and you won't be the last. For *you*, there may be nothing I could say today that would make you think any differently, and you're counting down the moments until I step aside and let the remainder of the service occur so Trevor can be laid to rest. For *you*, perhaps all I can do is pray that one day you'll hear a knock and answer it...that you'll find the one and only thing that will ever fill that void you've always known you have."

Long pause this time.

"I also know that many of you *are* believers. And I know for you, today may be even *harder*. You see, I know that so many of you have been ardently praying for Trevor these last few months—praying for a miracle from God and from modern medicine in the form of a new heart. For you, you *know* God. And God knows you. And yet...you sit here today mourning loss rather than celebrating a miracle, and maybe it feels like the God you know and the God who knows you wasn't listening. How else could we have gotten to this place today?"

Even longer pause. Sip of water.

"And now, whichever group you sit in, you're looking at me and waiting for me to give you the answer to the one question you all have—*why*? I'm sorry to disappoint every one of you, but I don't have that answer for you today. None of us do. You see, whether you believe in God or not, or you are somewhere in the middle, you must know that any god that would be fully comprehensible by our three-pound human brains—as much of a miracle as those three pounds truly *are*—would be such a *small* god. How would we ever be in awe of a god we can fully understand, predict...and *control*? No, our God is far *bigger* than that. The same God who put the stars into motion a billion light years away put the cells together that make up our three-pound brains that are capable of art, music, critical thinking, scientific reasoning...pediatric surgery...and love."

Another sip of water and a glance at Kelly, who had tears streaming down her cheeks.

"So, folks, that is why days like today are the hardest days in my work. Because I don't have the answer to the one question everyone has. Not today. No, only God has that answer. But might it be that we'll *all someday* know the answer to that question when we reunite once more? *That* is why I'm honored on days like this to point you all to God. While we won't know *why*, we can celebrate the life God breathed into Trevor Anderson forty years ago. That life would go on to improve or save so many young lives in his professional career and give life to two beautiful children. We can thank God for the special person Trevor was and the memories we'll always have of him, knowing we were better off having him with us on this earth for forty years than not at all. Because, while our prayers may *not* have been answered these last several months, *countless* prayers from folks in this very room and from folks you'll never know *were* answered in the form of Dr. Trevor Anderson's time with us. And, for that, we thank God."

With that, he nodded at the funeral director and slowly made his way back to his folding chair. The funeral director's soothing voice announced that there would be a series of speakers, starting with Trevor's brother, Randy.

Randy bravely spoke about growing up with Trevor, watching him fall in love with Kelly, and learning from him about parenting, schooling, sports, dating, and countless other things a man learns from a brother who is three years his senior. He did a beautiful job, better than I could have ever done in his position. When it appeared, his remarks were beautifully wrapped with a concluding bow, he hesitated to leave the lectern. He looked at his wife, then at the preacher, and continued.

"The so-called 'miracles of modern medicine' couldn't save my amazing big brother…but it isn't medicine I've come to doubt…it's miracles."

He collected his notes back into his suit coat pocket and returned to his seat, shaking and sobbing.

Next, the director of the surgery department at St. Stephen's, Dr. Minesh Gulpari, spoke glowingly and emotionally of Dr. Anderson's work as the head of pediatric surgery. He had a towering reputation as not only a gifted surgical tactician but also for exhibiting the absolute best bedside manner of any surgeon he'd ever encountered. The kids loved him. Parents loved him. He had a way of exuding calm confidence, mixed with sincere empathy. It was the reason the hospital had featured him on billboards and in social media posts.

Finally, Dr. Gulpari introduced a moderately dressed olive-skinned woman in her late thirties, Kara Abdo, to speak. She introduced her eight-year-old daughter Stella, sitting pensively in the second row, her jet-black hair pulled back tightly in a ponytail. Through tears—at times turning to sobs—she spoke of being asked by St. Stephen's to represent the hundreds of families in the area who had been touched by Dr. Anderson's work, how Stella would not be sitting there that day if it weren't for him identifying a rare condition, after so many others had missed it, that needed immediate surgical attention—and for the skill with which he executed that surgery late into the evening hours that same day. She reiterated Dr. Gulpari's words about the way Dr. Anderson made her and her daughter's father *feel* prior to and after the surgery. She closed with this: "Four years ago, we did not know what was wrong with our tiny four-year-old daughter, and we prayed to God every day to help us figure it out before something horrible happened. The minister today was right. When we sat with Dr. Anderson in that room at the hospital while Stella was being prepped for surgery, he put his hand on mine…and…I felt the *hand of God* on my shoulder. I knew in that moment that our prayers had been answered and everything would be okay. Thank you for listening to my family's story today. And thank you, especially to the Anderson family, for allowing me to speak on this sad day."

At last, the funeral director nodded to Randy, who turned to a group of men scattered in the rows behind the family. They all rose, moved to the casket, and prepared to take a handle. Dr. Anderson's family came forward and tearfully said their last goodbyes. With Kelly's help, little Owen placed his red, yellow, and blue superhero action figure into his dad's right hand before the curved door that was the large casket lid was slowly closed. The pallbearers each took hold and carried Dr. Anderson out the back door to the waiting hearse.

I decided to follow the line of flagged vehicles to the cemetery. I vacillated between staring blankly at the road ahead of me, lost in thought about the world without Dr. Trevor Anderson, and nervous energy leading my finger to rapidly flip through the car radio dial as I drove. I stopped flipping when I heard a rare but familiar banjo riff that made me smile and drift off into thoughts of Will.

A year before he moved from Colorado to Chicago, Ann and I flew out to visit him and ski the Rockies for the first time in our lives. He broke his ankle snowboarding two weeks before our arrival, but he made the best of it and played up the host role, even though he couldn't participate on the slopes. On our first night there, Will put on some kind of twangy banjo music while we hung out and chatted.

"What the *hell* are we listening to?" I teased him.

"What?" he defensively responded. "This is awesome. Haven't you seen this movie?"

"No. What movie?"

"*O Brother, Where Art Thou?*"

"Ah, nope. This isn't exactly the 50 Cent we were listening to on the way over here from the airport."

He shot back, "Man, you gotta open up to new stuff. We'll watch the movie some time, and you'll get it."

The next morning, I awoke to the beautiful smell of bacon and stumbled out of the bedroom toward the kitchen to find Will loading the movie into the DVD player.

"We'll watch it before we head to the slopes."

I honestly don't remember much of that movie. I guess it was supposed to be a modern take on *The Odyssey* or something. All I remember was that music. And, you know what? It grew on me. I never really paid much attention to the lyrics, and they're a bit hard to follow, but I jammed out to the Soggy Bottom Boys song on my way to the cemetery, wishing Will was riding shotgun with me, pretending to play the banjo, and cracking me up.

I am a man of constant sorrow
I've seen trouble all my day.
...

For six long years I've been in trouble
No pleasures here on earth I found
For in this world I'm bound to ramble
I have no friends to help me now.
...

For I'm bound to ride that northern railroad
Perhaps I'll die upon this train.
...

You can bury me in some deep valley
For many years where I may lay
Then you may learn to love another
While I am sleeping in my grave.
...

Maybe your friends think I'm just a stranger
My face you'll never see no more.
But there is one promise that is given
I'll meet you on God's golden shore.
(He'll meet you on God's golden shore).

It wasn't long into the drive—and shortly after coming back from my memory to the reality of navigating traffic—I realized we were driving to the two-hundred-acre cemetery visible from I-75 where my best friend lay waiting for our arrival.

What are the chances?

I pulled into the cemetery, about the thirtieth car in line to do so, parked along with the rest, and watched an endless stream of vehicles follow our lead. Spookily reminiscent, of course. A second such line I'd seen in only a few months. Or was it the fifth or sixth? I only hope to have enough impact in my time to warrant a caterpillar of cars *half* the length of Will Hogan's and Dr. Trevor Anderson's.

The remainder of the service went as you'd expect, with the pot-bellied "Gawd" preacher concluding with plenty of pregnant pauses and, "We therefore commit this body to the ground, earth to earth, ashes to ashes, dust to dust; in sure and certain hope of the resurrection to eternal life." He thanked those who weren't part of Dr. Anderson's immediate family for attending and politely made it clear that it was time for those of us who matched that description to depart.

I followed the rest of my kind toward the line of vehicles, most of us walking across Kelly Anderson's eyeline. She wrapped each of her arms around her kids and held them like they'd blow away if she didn't. A few blew her kisses. A few gave air hugs or prayer hand gestures. I nodded and looked her in the eyes. Of course, there was no indication of recognition on her part. Why would she know me? In her world, she'd never met me. There was no reason for us *to* have met. I remained in her eyes for longer than was probably comfortable for either of us. I had seen her tears before, as she had handed Alex and me the audio file of Will's beating heart in her husband's living chest. Naturally, this day's tears were different: tears for what *was*, not those of gratitude for delivery from what almost *had been*.

Kelly's new, different tears haunted me. The consciousness of my role in perhaps creating those tears was crushing. I lay awake that night, my own tears saturating my pillow.

He's been gone for months this time. What if the cycle stops right now?
What if this is it?
The four.
The other.
The lives orbiting Trevor Anderson's life and career.
It's all too much.
What if this is it?
What if this is the final way we lose Will?
What if this is it?
What if this is the end of the story?
What if this is it?
What if this is it?

SAVING WILL

No.
No. It must *repeat.*
Will must *come back.*
He just has to.
His life must end the way it did before.
The first time.
The real time?
For the five.
That was the way it was supposed *to happen.*
None of this now feels right.
It can't be.
This is all wrong.
There is nothing I can do to save Will.
There is nothing I should *do to save Will.*

I rolled out of bed and stood. My knees got weak, my legs wobbled, and I fell to the ground like my limbs had been kicked out from under me. I leaned my forehead against the dark wood bed frame, to which I also clung with the clenched fingers of both hands.

And for the first time since Will's death, I prayed.

It was more like begging.

I begged God to bring him back just once more, to continue this heart-wrenching cycle, not so that I might attempt to save him again, but so I could finally let him go. This had become all wrong, and I asked God to make it right again. I gave up. I gave it all up. I was done fighting and trying—vainly, *destructively*—to control the situation. I had to give it up—for the five, for my sanity. Some of the pleading words were mine; others came from some other place. I closed my prayer with words I'd heard every time Ann, and I attended a church service: "Thy kingdom come, *thy* will be done."

Silence.

Broken by Ann's voice: "Honey?"

"Hmmm…huh?"

"Are you okay?"

"Yeah, yes. I'm good," my voice cracked. I sniffled, only half-attempting to hide the tears and snot flowing from my face.

From her position lying in bed, she reached down and stroked the back of my neck.

"That was a beautiful and…confusing prayer," she added gently.

That was out loud?

"Ugh. I, um…didn't realize. I thought that was in my head."

"Well, I've always been taught it's better to pray out loud anyway, so that's good you did that." She paused. "What was all the stuff about bringing Will back one more time so he could die the right way? Are you okay? I mean, do you think it's time you talked to a professional and got some help?"

Not this again.

"No. It's all too much. It's all too much to explain, and you'll think I'm completely crazy. Can we just let it go? I'm not even sure what could possibly come from this."

"God hears our prayers, RJ."

"I sure hope so, Ann."

I climbed back into bed and fell asleep, holding her hand.

*****

It was a familiar scene. I was sitting at a picnic table at the small beach park near Ann's parents' house. There were several unknown people sitting around the table. Though I sat with them, I sat above them a bit, so I looked down on them. Across from me again sat Will. But I wasn't really me, of course. I was *Jesus*.

Like before, I just *was*, and somehow, I *knew* I was, and I was looking (slightly down) at Will, and we spoke to each other, but we didn't speak words. As we communicated and I looked at him, I again felt warm *throughout* my being. Again, I knew Will and the other faceless beings around the table in an all-encompassing way, light years beyond what words on a page could tell. I knew Will and the rest of them better than they knew themselves—better than anyone *could* possibly know *anything*. In real time, some layer of my consciousness recognized this dream as a rerun.

And then, a plot twist. I—as all-knowing Jesus—gradually looked away from Will and along the row of nondescript faces seated at the table until I reached a familiar face at the foot of the table. That feeling of warmth washed over me—as Jesus. And it penetrated the young man at the end of the table; I could feel it *through* him. Our faces met. He looked broken. Not his face per se. His whole *being*. His head bowed slightly, his eyes unhurriedly closed, then just-as-unhurriedly reopened, and then his face reengaged with mine. And when he lifted his face back to mine and connected, I simply knew he wasn't broken any longer. He exhaled, and his shoulders dropped. His terse brow relaxed. His face radiated peace. It was the most familiar face in the world. It was my own.

*****

Nothing gets the heart rate up faster than a blaring phone in the middle of the night. I jolted upright and swung around to answer it, cursing under my breath for forgetting to silence my flip phone ringer prior to lying down and hopeful that Ann would be able to fall back asleep in preparation for her early morning wake-up for work. I tried to grab the Nokia off the nightstand, but it wasn't there. The nightstand, I mean. I found the screaming phone unplugged and on the carpeted floor next to the bed.

Will Hogan.

This time I took an extra breath and feebly attempted to gain my composure before answering.

"Hello?"

"Yo! Did I wake you from your beauty sleep?"

"Hmmm? Ha. Yeah, I guess so. I forgot to mute my ringer. You're…"

"Aren't you supposed to be partying it up with the guys to celebrate whooping some younger guys' asses on the soccer field?"

"Huh?"

"You're in Petoskey for the tournament, right?"

As my eyes adjusted to the darkness, I scanned my surroundings. No Ann. Air mattress on the floor of a mostly empty bedroom. I *was* in Petoskey for the tournament. It was late Saturday, June 19, the night of the voicemail he left me, telling me Ann loved me when I didn't answer the first time—the one I had absently deleted.

"Yeah. I'm in Petoskey."

"You alright, dude?"

"Yeah, just waking up a bit disoriented. It's great to hear your voice though, Will."

"Haha. Likewise, buddy. Even if you do sound a bit loopy."

"Yeah. I wasn't sure if…" I tapered off into mutual silence.

"Well, anyway, just checking in before I head home tomorrow. I've got most of my packing done, will do the finishing touches in the morning, am borrowing my parents' Tahoe, and will be hitting the road sometime midmorning if everything goes according to plan. You still up for getting together Monday night?"

"Yes. That would be good. That…*will* be good."

"Sweet. You heading over to your folks' place for Father's Day tomorrow?"

"Yeah. Sometime in the afternoon."

"Very good. Tell them I said 'hi' and tell your dad I said 'Happy Father's Day.'"

"Will do. Same…Same to your parents and your dad, okay?"

"Absolutely. Looking forward to being back in 'The D' to be around to celebrate these days."

My voice cracked. "Yeah, that'll be nice. I know…I know they miss you, man."

"Yep. Well, I'll let you get back to sleep, princess, and I'll see ya Monday."

"Yeah, okay, buddy. Drive carefully. I'll…" I cleared my throat. "I'll see you soon, okay?"

"Cool, cool."

*****

As you know, the long drive home from Petoskey is mainly flat roads, but they might as well have been hilly that Sunday, as my mind raced, and I rode up and down through sadness, anticipation, relief, regret, guilt, and bracing for impact like one does when about to rip a bandage off of hairy skin.

I got home in time to hug Ann closely before she left for her parents' house. Rather than nap, I sat up stiffly on the couch, watching that same US Open final round, incessantly sipping water for reasons beyond me, and holding my phone. Though my eyes watched the green scene at Shinnecock Hills Golf Club on the TV, my head and heart ran through my time in this world with Will. I smiled and cried as I thought about the way he strutted around Mitchel College's campus in our first year. Some people were cool without trying; Will was cool *because* he wasn't trying. Many people showed care for others in a loud, visible way so as many people as possible would know they were caring for others. Will cared for others in a private, almost disguised way because he felt helping someone else should be done for the sake of it alone. Most people did enough in their long lives to be considered best friends by a few; Will did enough in twenty-six years to be called a best friend by more people than any of us "best friends" even knew.

I saw him wearing the Jim's Snack Shack hairnet and seemingly loving it and giving zero care about what anyone else thought about it or him wearing it. I heard his voice calling a parking attendant by her first name. I saw Denny, the custodian, tipping his cap across the central campus courtyard to an enthusiastic young man shouting his name. I heard his mischievous laugh as he shaved an eight in his own arm. I saw him sitting at the base of a mountain with a broken ankle, patiently and gladly watching Ann and me ski the Rockies for the first time. I heard his voicemail telling me he was just calling to tell me Ann loved me.

Then I saw the SUV rolling, everything he owned, including his life, spreading across I-94, and the blood. I saw his sandals flying off his feet as the drunk ran him down and continued on into the dark night. I saw the closed casket, not the open one.

Then an ounce of hope—an epiphany of what this could have been.

What if he's back and survives on his own this time, without me doing anything?

What if this whole thing was some kind of test for me?

Maybe somehow this will be different in a good way for everyone involved.

Then the call came.

Right on time.

The beginning of the answer to some people's prayers.

The beginning of hell for many others.

The end of purgatory for me.

"The police just came to our house," she said, not crying but obviously shaken and speaking in short bursts. "Will's been in an accident. They say it might be pretty bad. We are on our way to the hospital now. He's unconscious. I'm freaking out right now. He's my baby, RJ. I called you and Marcus. You guys tell everyone else. Tell them to pray. Just tell them to pray."

"I will be praying; Mrs. H. Everything is…going to work out. I will call people and tell them to pray."

I made the brutal phone calls again, without tears this time. It's not that I wasn't sad. I was. It's that things were happening in an *orderly* way—as strange as that sounds—the *right* way. The way it was *supposed* to happen. As sad as it was, it was the answer to my prayer. So, my calls were factual, and I asked people to pray. I came over to see you and Mom for Father's Day and shared the news with you as well. I didn't bother asking you to pray.

The next day, after work, Ann and I went to the hospital. Hugs, tears, stories, and explaining the number shaved in his arm. Hearing family talk about what it would be like when he came out of the coma. Quietly agreeing. Joining them in prayer. Having a different conversation with God. We were there almost every night that week, missing Saturday to attend a wedding at which Will was supposed to be a groomsman with me in Northern Michigan.

The following Monday, I was with Terrance at the hospital in Dearborn again. I was not sure why I didn't call in sick that day. Maybe I was trying to keep everything in order to ensure everything went the way it was supposed to—some last crumb of believing I had *some* control over a situation that had long since escaped my grip. The texts and calls came, and I returned Alex's call.

He didn't say hello. He picked up and, through sobs, told me that Will was brain dead. "He was supposed to make it," Alex cried. "He was supposed to live. This wasn't supposed to happen. I can't believe this is happening."

"I am so, so sorry, Alex," my splintered voice replied. "You're right, man. It wasn't supposed to happen." I no longer believed these words, a fact not important for what needed to be said to a brother in shock.

After hearing Terrance's story of a too-young death, I made my way to the parking deck to call Ann. I sobbed when I called her, likely because I was feeling empathy for her hearing of Will's death for the first time. Likely, too, because I always let my guard down with her, and this was starting to feel final—which was tough to swallow.

We had our parking lot meetup, an embrace, and more tears. She drove us to the hospital while I made the final phone calls to deliver the horrific news. We met the Hogans with tears and hugs in the familiar family waiting area. After several minutes, we were all asked to leave the room so Mr. and Mrs. H could meet with Gift of Life. Through the glass, I watched them sign the paperwork.

Alex caught my gaze and muttered under his breath, "I guess there are five organ donations that can be made, so…" He nodded as his point trailed off into the sterile hospital air.

After a hushed moment, his sister added to no one in particular, "kidney, heart, cornea, liver, and pancreas."

Those "parts" carried a different meaning for me than anyone else in the room, and more than they ever had before. As Will's parents breathlessly sat across from a man and woman holding clipboards with forms awaiting signatures, they heard "kidney"; I heard Gabi. They saw "heart"; I saw Dr. Anderson, Kelly's grateful tears, giggling kids chasing each other at a park, and countless future little patients. They thought "cornea"; I thought of Malcom's watchful eye over Kameron's violin. They signed off to donate Will's liver; I thought of how Keith's family had written him off and the chance he now had to transform these relationships. They contemplated the impact of his pancreas; I knew we'd never know, but I also knew a day may come when we all might consider it a gift to receive every person in our world as if he or she entered our lives with that important piece of Will in tow.

*****

We pulled into the funeral home's same hot blacktop parking lot, whose smell was my purgatory aromatic backdrop. Ann parked in the same spot she always had, because I guess that's just where she would have always decided to park for Will's funeral. Details like this still fascinated me in the depths of my pain and suspected delusion.

Why would a detail like that always be the same? Why is her brain hard-wired to park in that same damn spot every time? If I convince her to park in a different spot, will it change anything?

"Hey, don't park so close to the building this time."

"This time?"

"I...I meant, just, I'd like to stretch my legs a bit before we have to go sit in there. Can you park along that back wall on the other side of the lot?"

She maintained eye contact for an extra-concerned extra beat, then silently put the car in reverse and satisfied my request. After pulling into a section shaded with oak trees where no other mourners had yet parked and putting the car in park, she turned to me and squeezed my hand. Tears welled up in her eyes. I reminded myself that, despite the repeated pain I had endured with each of Will's deaths, her pain was new. It was fresh and raw. While I mourned my lack of ability to save him, she simply mourned his death—the way I had the first time, which seemed so long ago by that point. It made me stop thinking about my own grief for a moment and realize she too was in pain.

I squeezed her hand back and whispered, "I'm sorry."

"For what?"

"For this being all about me, I know you are gonna miss him too. You've been through a lot this week yourself, while you've been there for me. I'm sorry. I love you. Thank you."

We hugged and sniffled softly together across her Escape's middle console. When we released and each grabbed a tissue and tried to compose ourselves, we both stared straight ahead at the gray cinderblock wall at the front bumper of the vehicle. I locked in on the one fleck of green on the five-foot-tall barrier. It was a tree. It looked to be a tiny oak sapling, growing out of the side of a solid parking lot barricade. There was life coming out of seemingly impossible nothingness—perhaps from a spot of dirt lodged into the blah-colored wall in the back part of a funeral home parking lot at a busy intersection in metro Detroit. It just found a way.

I stiffened my spine and turned to Ann. "You ready?" I asked.

She looked at me with a "that was my line" look and nodded.

We walked across the parking lot, running into no fewer than three other college friends getting out of their cars, one of whom was Will's freshman year roommate who traveled from Hawaii to be there. Hugs were exchanged, tears were shed, and the usual things were said. We wished we could have this reunion just because, not because of this cause. Etcetera. We found our way through the double doors and toward the guest book.

As I wandered down the brightly lit, potpourri-scented hallway toward the entrance of the room where Will lay in his casket, I paused to watch the slideshow set to music playing on the TV at the end of the hall. A man in his sixties turned to another and said, "It is such a blessing that five other people were able to benefit from Will's organ donation." Ann squeezed my hand, and I could feel her looking up at me while I turned my head toward the men. She braced for my outrage at such a comment. I stared briefly, turned to my bride, and smiled. "He's right, you know."

Walking past the photo boards, which would somehow find their way to a permanent place in our basement many years later,

SAVING WILL

Will's brother-in-law-to-be pulled me aside right on cue to ask me to be a pallbearer. "It would be my honor."

After we viewed the last photo board, we found ourselves yet again standing over my deceased best friend—the high school baseball hat, of course, hiding his swollen head. Rather than lament mediocre last words, a missed phone call, or a deleted voicemail, my grief was joined by thankfulness for having had multiple second chances at last moments with Will.

The funeral director gave his instructions for everyone to find a seat, and somehow we landed in the same middle section we had so often found before. The same planned speeches were given. Will's brother-in-law-to-be was excellent, of course, and then the funeral director opened the podium to anyone else who wanted to say anything, which was met with the same painful silence, and I felt the same eyes on me.

I stood up.

Everyone looked. I floated forward to the podium. I cry at movies and even the occasional professional sports moment, so I'm not sure what gave me composure for this. It was time, I guess. This time, I would get it right.

"Thank you for the opportunity to speak today. I have known Will for eight years, but it seems much...much longer. When we pledged a fraternity together during our freshman year in college, we memorized a passage written by John Walter Wayland in 1899. It goes like this:

> The True Gentleman is the man whose conduct proceeds from good will and an acute sense of propriety, and whose self-control is equal to all emergencies; who does not make the poor man conscious of his poverty, the obscure man of his obscurity, or any man of his inferiority or deformity; who is himself humbled if necessity compels him to humble another; who does not flatter wealth, cringe before power, or boast of his own

> possessions or achievements; who speaks with frankness but always with sincerity and sympathy; whose deed follows his word; who thinks of the rights and feelings of others, rather than his own; and who appears well in any company, a man with whom honor is sacred and virtue safe.

"While perhaps no man has ever lived up to the distinction of being a true gentleman, no man has ever come closer than Will Hogan. I suspect for those of you hearing these words for the first time, you thought of examples or stories from Will's life where he lived up to this distinction. I know I'll never hear these words the same way again.

"Today is a sad day. I am sad. We are all profoundly sad. In the days and weeks to come, we'll all think about Will constantly. At some point, I suspect we'll go from thinking about him every minute to every hour, then every day, or at least every week. To the Hogan family, I know it will be different for you. It will likely never stop being every day, and for you, I pray for peace. For all of us, I suspect the times we do think of him will be very sad at first, and we will forever mourn losing him so soon. But I also suspect that as the years go on, when we hear a song, talk to a mutual friend, or come across a photo that reminds us of Will, we will smile. Maybe even laugh. Okay, knowing the stories we have, we will *probably* laugh. That's hard for all of us to think about now, but I think we'll be sad and happy at the same time: sad that he's gone and happy that we had the time we did. Happy that we had the friend, son, brother, or uncle we had.

"Which brings me to my last point. Again, I'll say I am sad. We are all profoundly sad. At the same time, there are five families today thanking God for their second chance at life. Perhaps a new liver that will allow someone to not only survive, but change the way life and life's relationships look. Perhaps a new kidney that will allow someone to be the first in a family to finish college, write music, and maybe fall in love. Perhaps new eyesight for someone whose brushes with fame pale in comparison to the simple pleasure of seeing a small family sip lemonade around a patio table. Perhaps a new heart for someone with a heart for family and for serving others...or saving others. Perhaps a new pancreas for someone you know. Or someone you don't know.

"I know that every one of you sitting here today would give anything to turn back time and save Will. I have thought about that... more than you'll ever know these last...few days. But I've decided *today* to let that go. I am not going to save Will. I am going to *celebrate* Will. I am going to mourn his passing but celebrate his life and the life he gifted others in his last act on this earth. None of us are likely to ever meet any of them, but that's okay. In fact, it may be a blessing. Here's why. The grocery clerk in the checkout line may have Will's kidney. Your child's surgeon may have Will's heart. The person who cut you off in rush hour traffic may have Will's liver. And because we don't *know* who has a piece of Will inside them, keeping them going every day, maybe we'll treat everyone we come across as if they *do*. Maybe that is his last gift to all of *us*. Maybe that's the piece of Will *we* get to carry around inside of *us* for the rest of our days."

Turning to the casket I finished with, "I love you, brother. I'll see you soon, okay?"

*****

When I stood beside the hole in the ground that would soon forever house my best friend's remains, I stared at—as I had before—the miles-long line of cars. Rather than cars this time, I saw people. Every person in every one of those vehicles was touched by Will's life. It made me want to be a better person. It made me ask myself what I needed to do in my life to earn a line of vehicles that long—not for some sort of posthumous pride, but for impacting those I would someday leave behind.

If he did this in twenty-six years, what can I do with whatever time I'll have?

The minister once again delivered words to the large crowd in preparation for laying Will in the ground. Once the words were spoken, everyone other than his immediate family was gently asked to leave. As I had every other time, I felt strange walking away at that time. Will *felt* like immediate family, and it would have felt somehow more permanent to see his casket lowered into the ground. But I also understood.

Ann again took the wheel of the Escape; we buckled up, held hands, and quietly served as one of the lead vehicles for the long and winding road toward the cemetery exit. On the three-mile drive home, I stared out the passenger-side window and thought about everything Will taught me in the eight years I'd known him. I also thought about Denny, the custodian, giving a nod of his cap across campus, and Jessie, the little brother mentee, waving his lacrosse stick. Just as the images of these changed lives played in the middle distance of my gaze, we slowly passed a city park. There, quickly circling a picnic table, was a red-haired boy squealing and chasing his shrieking older sister, while two parents watched and laughed.

I looked straight ahead in time to see us pass through a yellow light. I managed a smile, kissed the index and middle fingers on my right hand, then touched the car's ceiling and squeezed Ann's hand as she steered the car south to head home.

*****

Well, that's about it. I know that was a lot. It appears my fear that this letter would turn into a book was well-founded. I don't know which of these realities you experienced. I imagine it was the last one because that's the one that "stuck" and the only one anyone else has ever acknowledged now, thirteen years later. I'm sure you could confirm this by acknowledging whether you heard me speak at his funeral or not. We never really talked about it.

Of course, Will never came back after that. I braced myself for it, less so as the months—and certainly years—drove on. I've never completely lost the anticipation of getting to see him again. But now I've grown sure that when, not if, I next see him, it will be in a different way.

SAVING WILL

I've had plenty of reminders of him over the years—occurrences I now chalk up to God reminding me about Will or maybe Will looking out for me from afar. I'll give you one example. About a year after he was gone for good, Ann and I attended a charity wine tasting event. The plan was to participate in the wine tasting, then stick around after with a small group of friends for dinner and conversation—thus giving me, as our driver, plenty of time to let any effects of the wine tasting work their way out of my system before getting behind the wheel. Ann's body had other plans. About forty-five minutes after the wine tasting portion of the evening ended, she vomited in the ladies' restroom. She was sick and likely embarrassed, and she wanted to get home immediately. These days, I would open an app on my phone, and a car would pick us up in minutes. Back then, I probably could have called a cab, but instead, I chugged some water, went, and got the car. I was by no means drunk—not even close. But I was also by no means totally dry—just enough to be easily distracted.

Will would have strangled me, Dad. We shared a mutual intolerance for drinking and driving from the time we met. Oddly, this shared disdain sprung from the same historical event that occurred before we even met. I'm sure you remember that Mark Simpson, who I played travel soccer with as a kid, was killed—along with two fellow high school classmates—by a drunk driver during his senior year. What you might not know is that Will's friend, Stacy, was one of those fellow high school classmates. Weird, huh? We referenced them often, and when we went out, we always decided in advance who was going to drive home. So, yeah, Will would not have approved of my decision after the wine tasting, and if he'd been there, he wouldn't have let it happen.

Ten minutes into our drive, we were close to home. I was doing fine navigating the vehicle while Ann sat with a plastic shopping bag in her lap in case she got sick again. Having just passed Will's cemetery on the right, I began to merge to the right exit lane of the highway, only to see ahead and to the left on the highway we were just exiting several flashing police and ambulance lights. I looked left as I merged right and commented to Ann, "I wonder what's going on up there."

As I looked over to her for a response, I saw just how close I came to sideswiping a presumably abandoned vehicle on the shoulder of the long and gradual exit. The hair on my neck stood up, thinking about how close we came to my distraction causing an accident. Before those hairs had a chance to sit back down, the vehicle now in my rearview mirror had its lights on and roared up on my tail with blue and red lights flashing. Terror ran through me. The guy who hated when people drove drunk was now getting pulled over with wine in my system and a sick wife sitting next to me.

I made my way into an office building parking lot where Officer Rodriguez, who greeted me at my window, was not happy.

"Do you realize how close you came to hitting me back there?"

"Yes. I'm sorry, I got distracted by the accident up ahead."

"Have you been drinking tonight, sir?"

"We were at a charity wine tasting event and my wife got sick, so we left way earlier than we planned. I had wine. It's hard to say how much because it wasn't by the glass. But I'm not drunk."

"I'm gonna need your license and registration, sir."

As he walked back to his unmarked vehicle, with lights flashing and an incredibly bright search light blasting through my back window, Ann said, "I'm so sorry. This is all my fault."

"No. I should have found a different way."

He reapproached my car. "Sir, I'm going to ask you to step out of the vehicle. Have you ever participated in a field sobriety test?"

"No, sir."

"Based on the near accident back there and the fact that you've been drinking, we are going to conduct that test now."

I've been back to that parking lot years later, in the middle of the day, as sober as the day I was born, and I can confidently tell you that the concrete is slanted. It's on a slight hill. Looking back on it, I can't believe anyone would do a test like that on such an uneven surface, but maybe he was hoping to meet his quota by the end of the month or something. I went through the tests quite well, both physically, despite that crooked ground, and mentally, counting backward from one hundred by sevens until he got bored. He also had me blow into a breathalyzer. As I blew into the contraption, another police vehicle arrived on the scene. He looked down at the results and then over his shoulder to his colleague, who was walking up to join him.

His name badge read Officer Peter Williamson.

You might remember that name because I had known him from seventh grade through the end of high school, played Nintendo at his house, and went fishing with him and his police officer dad. He immediately said hello to me in a way that acknowledged the unfortunate circumstances of our meeting. Once I apologetically explained the story of my evening to Pete and the officer I almost hit, Pete instructed me to stay by my car, and the two men walked back to his squad car to conference.

During their conversation, I stared at the ground and shook my head, as I remembered that it had been only eight months prior when I witnessed a motorcycle accident only two miles south of the spot I stood, called 911, and met with the first officer on the scene—my junior high school buddy, Pete Williamson. This time we were meeting under very different circumstances—too crazy to even make up.

As the men turned back toward me, my eyes locked in on my old friend's name badge. I swear the "Will" in Williamson glowed for a second. Maybe it was the high-powered spotlight catching it just the right way. Whatever the reason, as they walked toward me, I felt Will's presence with me.

Officer Rodriguez spoke first. "Well, your blood alcohol content puts you right near the border for going to jail. I know you have no history of this, and I understand that you had unforeseen circumstances tonight, so we're going to let you off with a warning."

My heart raced. Pete pursed his lips, nodded his head down, and added, "Yeah, RJ, just be safe tonight. How far do you have left to get home?"

"Literally less than a mile."

"Okay, just take it easy and be safe the rest of the way. And next time, call a cab, okay?"

"Thank you both. There won't be a next time. I can promise you that."

With that, Pete and I gave a nod of recognition.

It was good to see you, even though this was weird.

I sat back in the driver's seat and looked into Ann's tear-filled eyes. Keeping myself together, I drove the most careful mile of my life back to our condo, plopped down on the couch next to her and her just-in-case plastic bag, and broke down. I cried because of how close I'd come to having my life derailed. A DUI would have likely cost me my job, given that I operated a company vehicle every day. An accident, of course, would have been much worse. Naturally, I regretted putting us in that position. I also cried because I couldn't get the image of that name badge shining "Will" right into my eyes as it *happened* the officer I befriended in junior high school, who *happened* to be the first backup call, turned to deliver my get-out-of-jail-free card. That badge *happened* to shine the name of my deceased best friend, who *happened* to have shared a distaste for driving after having drank alcohol, due in large part to losing his high school friend—who *happened* to be in the same car with my childhood soccer teammate—to a drunk driver.

Yeah, that *happened*.

That was just *one* of the many times it felt like Will was still with me in some way.

Or maybe that was one of the many times I was simply *begging* for that to be the case.

He's come to me in smaller ways, too, like seeing someone out of the corner of my eye who looks like him and getting excited, just to be let down. Or the time someone carved the initials WEH into a tree at the beach. Or every time I catch myself saying, "Cool, cool."

In fact, Will helped me finish writing this letter. I'll explain.

I had talked to my boys a lot about Will over the years, so they knew who he was and had asked questions about him occasionally. At a time, when the words to this note I felt pulled to write you seemed to drip rather than gush, and I realized it was growing long and I didn't know how or why to finish it, I showed them a skiing photo of me,

Ann, and Will at the base of the mountain from when we went out to visit him. As they asked questions about Will's life, I suddenly remembered that I had put his obituary behind the photo in the frame. I got it out and read it aloud to them. They didn't say much, likely a bit uncomfortable getting to know Daddy's dead friend better. Then I found something I had zero recollection of stashing in the frame. Behind the obituary was a check Will wrote to me for $125, dated the night before my wedding, and with the word "Tux" in the notes section. (Will wrote a lot of checks for wedding tuxes in his short life.)

And, of course, there was his signature on the bottom.

Wow.

I brushed my thumb over the ink.

Will actually wrote *these words and signed his name just weeks before his death.*

It was well over a decade later, and somehow holding this check in my hand that he had once handed me and seeing his handwriting from the last month of his life made him come to life again for a moment. He died before I had time to cash it. I don't remember putting it in that frame, but I'm glad I did. It was a gift many years later. It inspired me to continue to put these words to paper.

*****

As I get to a point where I'm not sure what else to write down, I now must determine *why* I even wrote you this letter. It felt good to write this all down, but why did I choose to write this all down *for you*? Perhaps I needed you to see the pain I went through and the faith journey I've been on so you could know what's possible. I don't know.

I know you've been hurt by "church." But the bad acts of people professing to represent God are the bad acts of *people*, not of God. Since not long after His death and resurrection, people have misunderstood and misused Jesus to gain power and hold down or shame others, but that's not what He was about. Love. That's it. He was about love, Dad. 1. Love God. 2. Love others *as much as you love yourself.* To love, we must forgive. I know you're holding onto a lot, and any rational person would say you're justified. Maybe Jesus's followers aren't rational because He even taught us to love *our enemies*. That's about the hardest thing to do, but if there's anything I've learned from what I've finally revealed to you in these pages, it is that appreciating what we have, accepting our reality, loving others, letting go, and embracing forgiveness is the most freeing way to attack each day of our lives.

How sure am I that God exists? How sure am I that Will lives somewhere in some way, like heaven? About as sure as one can be about such things. The beautiful reality I now own is that I will see him again, and I'm not afraid of that day; I await it. I crave it. Until then, I will cherish my life as I never would have if not for Will, and I will relish from afar the lives Will gave those who carry a piece of him with them every day. As Dr. Trevor Anderson holds a finger to his pulse and thanks Will for it each morning, I tussle the tops of my boys' heads and feel every hair differently, knowing that Will never had a chance to do such a thing with kids of his own. And the God Gabi Dominguez's family thanks each day for her kidney is the same God I originally cursed every day after Will's death. The God I cursed every day is the same God who gave me those boys whose hair I now get to tussle. Settling into this understanding is not easy.

I don't know exactly when I'll give this letter to you, but I'm sure I'll find the right time. So you're probably reading this sitting in an airport, on a plane, on your couch, or maybe on a lounge chair near the water somewhere, and I'm sure if you're still reading this, you've been asking yourself many questions.

"Did this really happen?"

"Was this some sort of mental breakdown?"

"Did he just plain make this all up?"

All fair questions, the same I've asked myself more times than I can count, and I've given up trying to figure it out. But perhaps I'll answer all these questions with a question back to you.

Would it matter?

SAVING WILL

Perhaps from the darkness of despair comes the light of understanding. Perhaps from the complex razor's edge of insanity comes a sound conclusion. Perhaps the harder we try to hold on to something—someone, some idea—the more it oozes out of our grasp. Perhaps from the maniacal fever dreams of a soul so deeply hurting comes the one thing we all really thirst for—peace.

I'm glad I found it, and I hope you do too.

RJ

*****

Dear Reader,

The preceding pages were found typed, stapled, and packed into an 8.5" × 11" manila envelope in the coffin of a deceased man in Metro Detroit. Against normal protocol, and for reasons not currently understood, the envelope was removed and saved prior to cremation. Sometime later, the pages were anonymously delivered to the publisher with a note explaining their origin. It should be noted that after the final typed words, these handwritten sentences lay in blue ink:

> *I'm sorry it is in death that this story finally gets communicated. I'm sorry we couldn't have a conversation about this while we were together on this earth. Perhaps we'll have another chance.*

The End

DISCUSSION QUESTIONS

1. Do you know, or have you ever known, someone like Will Hogan? Talk about him or her.
2. Have you ever lost someone you loved at a young age? Talk about him or her if you are comfortable doing so.
3. RJ describes how he felt when Terrance consoled him by discussing a loss he suffered. Have you ever been consoled by someone who tries to say too much or tries to relate your loss to something in their life? How did that make you feel? Have you ever done that to someone else? How has this changed your approach to these situations, if at all?
4. This story is filled with imagery and symbolism. Discuss examples you observed and what meanings you perceived from them.
5. Dreams play an important role in this story. Discuss the meaning of the "lambs and trees" dream. Discuss the importance of RJ's other dreams. Have you been "visited" by deceased friends or relatives in dreams? Discuss examples and possible meanings for your dreams, if any. The Bible describes numerous examples of God delivering messages to people via dreams (Genesis 40, Daniel 4, Matthew 1:18–24, and Matthew 27:19, to name a few). What are your thoughts on that? Does God still do this today?
6. What are your thoughts on organ donation? If you are comfortable, share your own organ donor status. If you aren't sure, check your driver's license if you have one. Have you ever known someone who donated or received an organ donation? Discuss.

7. Have you or anyone you've known been hurt by "the church" or any religious organization? As much as you are comfortable, discuss. Discuss the notion that your example or others may represent negative acts by *people*, not God. Discuss how you've seen people misrepresent God "in His name."
8. Discuss one of the major themes of the book—our own will vs. God's will. What are your thoughts on *free will* (you can control your destiny) vs. *determinism* (your fate is decided for you)? Is there an in-between option? Have you ever found yourself exerting your own will against what you perceive(d) to be God's will? Have you ever found yourself "on your knees," giving in to God's will as RJ does toward the end of the story?
9. Bad things happen to seemingly good people, like Will. Share your thoughts on this. If you believe in God, how or why does God allow this?
10. During Dr. Anderson's funeral, his brother says, "The so-called 'miracles of modern medicine' couldn't save my amazing big brother…but it isn't medicine I've come to doubt…it's miracles." Are faith and science at odds with each other? Can one believe in science *and* believe in miracles, God, a higher power, or the supernatural?
11. Discuss the end of the book. In whose coffin was this letter found? Discuss the meaning of the blue handwritten note included with the letter. Have you ever regretted not telling someone something until it was too late?
12. The book starts with RJ not knowing why he was writing this letter to his dad. At the end, he seemed to realize why he did it. Is there someone in your life you need to write to or reach out to? Is there a story you need to tell others? Do you need to do one of these things before it's too late?

About the Author

Ryan Webb lives in the Detroit area, where he was born and raised, with his wife and two sons. He is a lifelong writer who is being published for the first time with this debut novel. He has written Bible studies taught at large churches, as well as devotionals, poetry, and short stories. Webb earned his bachelor of arts in communication and business administration from Alma College and a master of business administration from the University of Michigan's Stephen M. Ross School of Business. He's worked full-time for the same Fortune 100 company since 2000.